Woodcuts

A Fairy Tale for Unwanted Children

Scott Thrower

Woodcuts

A Fairy Tale for Unwanted Children

Periodically Productions

ISBN 978-1-9995501-1-0 (paperback)
ISBN 978-1-9995501-0-3 (eBook)

Dedication

Thanks to Mom and Dad, who let me dream a little longer than conventional wisdom might recommend.

My gratitude also goes out to the Unwanted Children for so many more reasons than can fit on this page.

Table of Contents

The Library 1

The Queen.. 8

Breakfast 12

Time Passes 23

Discovered 34

Escape 40

The Kingdom... 47

Subjects 62

Gathering... 74

The Old King... 81

Siege 88

Endings 101

About the Author... 103

Foreword

In April of 2017, I started a podcast. I had already failed at this once, having spent a year corralling comedians to talk about old magazines that I found in used bookstores and internet searches for a handful of listeners who weren't that impressed.

This time, I had a better idea of what I wanted from podcasting. I wanted a challenge, and I wanted to do something that would stretch creative muscles that had been atrophying since university. Most of all, I wanted something I could do alone. Matching schedules with people is a special sort of hell, and for an introvert to be ring-leader of an hour-long conversation each week just left me empty.

I came up with the title first — Fairy Tales for Unwanted Children. I had just streamed *Into the Woods*, something that normally happens much earlier in any gay man's life, and I was in love. The tropes of the genre created a beautiful shorthand that allowed a writer to get in and out quickly. People knew this stuff, these witches and queens. They already had wishing wells and dragons ready to go, which made for perfect content for the short episodes I wanted to make. It was a rich vein to mine, and I thought it might be easier to coax a few people into listening.

I grew up reading fantasy novels, so these characters felt like home to me, and once I started writing fairy tales, I knew I wouldn't stop.

The shows were downloaded 622 times that first month, and I was ecstatic. It doubled the next month, and that second month's number tripled in the third. Soon the podcast will hit a half-million downloads, which is far beyond even my wildest hopes, and the numbers are just the start of it.

These fairy tales have been played for students in elementary schools and passed around PhD message boards. I've had the chance to speak at a conference and dial in for a college Q&A. People wear the logo as they go about their days and tell their friends to listen, and people I look up to in the podcasting world have championed the show. There have been nominations for a number of awards and also a win. I even think the podcast is partly responsible for the job I have today.

The best part though is the people. There is a social media group full of the nicest folk you could ever meet who want to talk about the show. Sometimes I wake up and find a notification on my phone from a listener who just had to reach out and tell me how it's impacted their lives, but I don't know that they realize how much it has impacted mine.

Woodcuts started as an experiment. The show mostly features stand-alone episodes, though characters sometimes reoccur. I was playing a game with some friends and introduced the idea of books that came alive, and when the game was over, I couldn't shake the idea. Soon after, I had an outline for three short episodes, but as I kept writing, they grew. All four episodes came out over a period of two weeks because the story just needed to be told. I felt like I was apologizing to the Unwanted Children the entire time for this diversion from stand-alone episodes, but I wasn't prepared for the force of the reaction as people fell in love with the story.

There were no plans to write a book this soon, but I owe the Unwanted Children a debt for all of their kind words and support, so here it is. The core of the story is the same as the one listeners originally heard, edited to fix the shortcomings that came from the backbreaking pace of the podcasting schedule and deepened in places I previously skimmed over. In all, this edition adds about 5,000 words and fixes three times as many.

I'm proud of this story, and I'm proud of the community that has formed around it and all of the other tales, even the terrible ones that sometimes slip through. I won't say it has been an easy journey, but your kindness and generosity got me here, and I am a better person for it.

I hope you enjoy reading this book at least half as much as I loved writing it.

Scott

The Library

nce upon a time, there was a small boy in a large castle who knew every nook and hideout the ancient building provided, from the tunnels to the outer wall to the secret way from the kitchen to the eastern tower. Some days, he spent more time inside the castle walls than out, searching for new and forgotten paths and rooms that were sealed away.

In fact, the only person who may have known the castle better was his mother the queen. She'd once grown up here too, but somehow he couldn't picture her squeezing through cracks around a fireplace or chasing a whistling wind through the brickwork. She was also much bigger than the boy, and he couldn't imagine she'd ever been small. Even looking past her massive dresses like silken bells and her crowns that scraped grooves into door frames, the queen radiated a grandeur that made even the largest rooms of the castle feel crowded.

The boy loved that his mother couldn't always find him in his secret ways and that even if she had, she couldn't follow. He always listened for her though. It wouldn't do to have anyone take an interest in his disappearances, and it was never good to attract the queen's anger. If provoked, she would tear the castle down brick by brick, and no darkened corner or hidden way could stop her. So, when he heard the queen's calls echoing through the castle walls, the boy suddenly appeared, and no one bothered asking how he arrived.

One quiet day, the boy tired of watching the soldiers on the wall and listening to the hum of the village beyond. Much of the army was out in the field. There were no knights to follow, and the fighting at the gates had been quiet for weeks on end. He considered visiting the kitchens to find someone his age, but the queen had put such a fear into the staff that even the most foolish was suddenly busy when the boy came to call. He thought about finding his stepfather for stories of the war, but the old man had been sickly as of late and dozed off before the good bits.

Finally, the boy found himself standing in the library, looking around at the thousand books and wondering if today might be the day he read. He'd done his best to avoid it. Tutors taught him how, but they never convinced him why. His stepfather frequently fell asleep in various chairs around the castle with a book on his chest, but the boy never saw a book compelling enough to keep the old man awake. His mother was always reading, but only from a single book—a thick, old tome about laws and lineage. The boy was so bored by the genre that he had never even spared it a thought.

The library was on the second floor of the oldest part of the castle and so tight with shelves it seemed small despite stretching the entire northern wall of the building. The shelving was ancient and heavy. When he was younger, he'd spent hours climbing them until the servants caught wind and put that adventure to an end. There was a rolling ladder, and the boy wondered if he had grown strong enough to wheel it out for a ride through the halls. He discarded the idea when the heavy casters sank into the carpet making it impossible for the small boy to budge.

He ran his finger along the spines as he walked through the warren of shelves, trying to decide on a book to read. There were books on animals both common and rare, books of poetry in flowing scripts that talked about love and loss, and even a small, dark shelf of medical oddities that prickled the back of the boy's neck.

He stopped for a while at a history book full of castles and catapults. For a long hour he studied the drawings and woodcuts and compared them with the devices atop the walls outside that sometimes slung fiery pitch and rocks but usually sat tediously still. Whenever he watched the real ones too closely, the queen would chastise him to mind his own business and his stepfather would say it was best not to know. In the books their usage was both clear and entirely dull, so soon he was off searching for a more interesting read with fewer angles and calculations to get in the way.

Then as the boy walked near the central fireplace, his trailing finger snagged on a book and pulled it from the shelf.

It landed on the thick carpet in a puff of dust and

opened itself in the middle. It was a slim book, barely more than a dozen pages. When he bent to pick it up, the text swirled and spun across the page and made the boy's eyes ache. Even though it was just writing on a page, it rang in his head like a bell. After slamming the book shut with a satisfying thunk, the boy looked at the cover and saw it too crawled about in a bewildering way.

When the boy was much younger, the castle hosted many visitors who spoke other languages, but they'd never affected him this same way. These diplomats hadn't spared the child any thought. Instead, they yelled at his mother or, far more likely, listened as she shouted back. He didn't remember when their visits stopped, but he knew why. He'd been on the wrong end of the queen's anger many times himself.

It wasn't that she didn't love him, he assumed; it's just that he always seemed to be in her way, even when she placed him there herself.

Now he wondered which of those visitors had spoken a language that wouldn't stay still and how they could have possibly learned to read it. Normal text was already a challenge, and that was when it sat still on the page. He tried to pin down a squiggle with the tip of his thumb. It vibrated there before darting away to hide on the spine, and any other attempts to catch something failed as the ink moved much faster.

Eventually, the swirling, changing book was too much. The boy slipped it back onto the shelf where it almost disappeared between two larger books, a textbook on math and a thick, handwritten diary. Even though he knew the moving book was there, he could only see a hint of it, so perhaps it had lain there for generations without ever being read until catching on his finger. None of the other books had so much of a hint of dust. The outline this one left on the carpet made the boy certain that the book had somehow avoided the servants who never missed anything. They simply didn't dare.

As he watched the book, which seemed to burrow its way back into the shadows, something moved on the shelf, slightly off to the right. The boy turned just in time to see a small shape pull itself back into the pages of the heavy diary, but he wasn't fooled. There had been a tiny, paper head watching him from the pages of the book—maybe a deer or a dog. For a moment, he tried to convince himself it was a living, breathing mouse, though he'd never seen one this far up in the castle.

The leather binding of the diary felt warm in his hands. It was a travelogue, and as the boy pulled it from the shelf and settled down upon the carpet with it in his lap, the book shifted atop him and emitted a scratchy sound of rustling paper. He held his breath until the noise stopped just to be sure he'd heard it and then creaked open the cover.

The book burst open, and tiny animals flooded from it and scurried away in a frenzy of crinkling. Each was a small likeness made of pages intricately folded until they galloped or slithered, flapped, climbed or swam through the air. Soon all that remained was the empty leather cover of the book and a regal figure still standing on the spine, calmly meeting the boy's surprised gaze.

It was a white stag, about eight inches tall with antlers that branched out like the arms of a snowflake. The stag had strong black lines of a woodcut and pale, milky skin, but it was also folded together from lines of text and pale empty margins. It was so intricately done that the boy couldn't read more than a few letters even along the stag's long, smooth back.

The other animals watched and shuffled from where they hid behind table legs and lanterns, corners and chairs, but the stag seemed content where it was. It raised its head and sniffed the air, but its eyes never left the boy.

Scared to move, the boy held his breath lest he frighten the creatures away. The animals might flee up the chimney or through the gaps in the windows, slide under the grand library doors into the hall or lose themselves among the rafters. Even if the castle workers found the boy nowhere near the library, they'd somehow blame him for the damaged book and the plague of paper, though that thought faded into the back of the boy's thoughts almost instantly.

Something interesting had happened at long last, and suddenly the world was new.

He'd never seen a book like this before, though he wasn't certain that this was unusual. It was a question he'd never considered before because everything in his life seemed very usual and unchanging, but shouldn't someone have told him about such a book? Shouldn't there have been a warning? Perhaps someone should have used this book to explain why anyone bothered reading at all.

His tutors had come to tears attempting to get the boy to embrace reading, but if they'd just said books like this existed, they couldn't have kept him away.

"So, the adults don't know about you," the boy decided, looking at the white stag upon his lap. He watched it breathe and listened to the faint crinkle it made as it did. "You're a secret that's just mine."

He smiled and reached out a hand, but he couldn't bring himself to touch the stag, and so it touched him. It leaned its head against his fingers, and he felt the warmth of its fur and the coolness of the paper, and both were true together.

The Queen

From that day on, the boy was always in the library. He knew secret ways to get there, so when he finished his breakfast in the kitchens, he just disappeared for the day. After his dinnertime chats with his stepfather, while the queen glowered at her letters and reports, he faded off into dark passages before dessert arrived. If he heard the servants calling for him due to one of the queen's whims, he made sure they found him far from the library so no one wondered about the prince's new love of reading.

His tutors had disappeared when the queen decided he was sufficiently bright and the children of the stables when she ruled he'd been wasting his time with commoners. No one could take the book away if no one knew it existed, and so this secret was guarded more carefully than anything else. The queen never wanted for him to have too much of anything, and the boy had wanted nothing as much as he wanted this book.

The book revealled the world. One day, the broad study table dripped from stem to stern with swamps. The pages unfolded into trees heavy with moss and trickling green water. Paper crocodiles swam languidly while the air buzzed with insects that rested on the boy's arm, and the white stag silently drew his attention to various points of interest. They stopped at a species of flower with their name printed upon their petals and events that rocked the expanse of the table. Forgotten towers sank into the muck, and explorers traversed it. A black star fell from the dome of the sky to make the swamp bubble away into a stretch of farmland. Eventually, a broad city grew at the table's centre with tall towers and houses and huts that spiralled out and away.

Later, the rug in front of the fire became an arctic tundra or the book unfolded to become a different city with more battlements and moats. Ultimately, that city decayed into ruins only to be reclaimed by a new people, filled with paper citizens who lived their lives in the shadow of a paper volcano that grew in the fading afternoon sun before exploding shortly before dinner and sweeping the library clean. The boy realized this was all the same place, just told over great spans of time.

Through it all, there was the stag who walked through the tabletop world, and the boy learned to follow it with his eye because wherever the stag went, something of import inevitably happened. The stag was there when armies marched and diseases spread, crops failed and coronations trumpeted with fanfare. Sometimes the stag would nudge a tiny figure who would turn in surprise and then look from the stag to the boy before speaking.

"The city of Loam was founded by knights of the order of King Kelmir of the Bright Plain. I was a stonemason, responsible for the maintenance of—" and the boy listened and learned. It took a month to memorize every story the book offered, but the ideas stayed in the boy's head in a way that the tutors' words never had.

There were also the writers. A traveller wrote the journal, someone who'd wandered for thousands of years or more and kept returning to the same place. The boy realized he saw through her eyes and yet still learned so little about her. He looked for her reflection in the paper windows and mirrors, the sheen of the rivers and rain, but she never appeared.

Instead, the white stag guided him, and the boy wondered if this was why he'd heard the cook once speak of a white stag while he'd crept behind the kitchen walls on one of his adventures. Her voice had been brittle in a way he'd never heard, and he'd strained to listen to what she said, but she lowered her voice as she continued. When he realized she was weeping, the boy crept away, no longer feeling it appropriate to be listening.

Of all the woodcuts and drawings, paintings and sketches from the book, the stag was his favourite, and some of the best afternoons involved lazily looking out the window with the stag nuzzling his hand as events played out around them.

When this book stopped offering anything new, the boy hunted the library, listening for that scratchy sound of paper in the other books and searching the tall shelves for movement. He found a few stray numbers encamped beneath a sofa, but they couldn't hold his attention as they arranged themselves into equations and charts. In the end, there were no other living books found.

Eventually, the boy realized that if he rearranged the books just right, he could hide that the travelogue was missing, and that night he slept with the savannah of a long-dead princess spread across his blankets while the white stag roamed his pillows. When he awoke in the early hours and heard the even steps of the queen pacing the halls, he spotted braver paper figures creeping towards the hallway door, and he motioned them back into the book for their own protection. The boy returned to sleep listening to the queen's pacing with the warm book beneath his pillow.

Breakfast

n the third morning of having the book in his room, the boy rose to find most of the pages had put themselves away. He looked around, but all he found was the white stag standing still beside the door and a whale by the window, warming its belly in the morning sun. When he touched the stag, the boy found no hint of heat, and the beast barely turned its head as it was raised for a closer inspection. The stag felt like paper instead of muscle and fur, and no matter how closely he listened, the boy couldn't hear the crinkle of the stag's breathing.

A surge of panic gripped his heart. Someone called from the hall that breakfast was ready, and the boy hurriedly tucked the whale back into the book and pulled on his clothing before slipping the stag into his top pocket and sliding the book away beneath a cabinet. Somehow he had to get back to the library. Whatever was happening to the book had not happened in the months they'd spent there, and it terrified him that a few nights away may have destroyed whatever charm had been working.

That morning, the servants made sure the boy looked smart by brushing down his cowlicked hair and adjusting his tunic just so. His heart thrummed in his chest because he knew it wouldn't be his usual breakfast at the long kitchen work table with the cooks bustling around him. No one cared what he wore to those breakfasts. Instead, the servants brought him to the dining room, where he sat with his fearsome mother to his left. To his right was his frazzled stepfather who shook his head ever so slightly. This was their signal that today was a day to be bland and forgettable, a day to avoid the attention of the queen.

She ate her eggs and toast surrounded by stacks of maps and letters, muttering between bites and trailing crumbs into her cleavage. Neither she nor his stepfather noticed as the boy ate as quickly as possible or that he then sat waiting anxiously for dismissal. The stag had barely shifted in his top pocket, neither for comfort nor breath, and the boy had to be firm with himself to keep from checking that it was even still there.

The only time the queen looked up was to glare at the boy when he nervously tapped a spoon against his plate. He froze under her gaze, thinking of the three special ways out of the dining room.

There was the fire grate which led to a sooty tunnel out into the grounds, but with a small fire burning, it would be tricky. There was a trap door in the floor that led to a significant drop ending in a cold, stone dungeon, and he wasn't entirely sure he could make it before being caught or reach the bottom without being hurt. Finally, there was a panel behind the long buffet that had come loose, behind which hid a narrow space he could still just shimmy through before climbing up to a floor tile in a linen closet on the second floor.

Fortunately, he needed none of these because as the queen raised an eyebrow and parted her lips to speak, the hall door opened and a guest stepped in. Suddenly the boy ceased to exist for the queen, and both he and his stepfather released sighs that had been burning in their chests.

The guest was a tall, middle-aged man in a borrowed suit whose face glowed from too much sun. The suit had never been fine but perhaps may have once been extravagant for someone of meagre means, though it was too broad in the shoulders and too short in the pants. The hat the man in the man's hands quivered such that the boy thought there was a rabbit inside it. A moment later, he realized there wasn't; the man's hands shook, which the boy found entirely understandable. Out in the hall, there was a clatter which made the man jump as a dozen armoured guards tried not to make any noise.

"Your Majesty," the man mumbled.

"I've heard you surrender," the queen interrupted, carefully turning maps over and unaware of the crumbs clinging to her chin.

The man shrank before her until his pants almost seemed the right length. He kept his eyes on the carpet as if the message he was delivering was written there to read, and he cleared his throat twice before any further sound emerged.

"We can't speak for everyone, of course," he hedged.

"But you speak for most," the queen insisted, "and most have changed their mind about usurping their rightful queen."

14

"We may not be most," the man replied, clearly wishing he could say anything else. He held his floppy felt hat like a shield, and the boy's gaze dropped to his plate. He didn't want to see any more.

"This kingdom has passed down in my family since time began," the queen said, patting the thick tome that was always by her side, perched in its regular spot to her left. "It is written."

In the boy's top pocket, the stag shifted, and he clapped a hand against his shirt so quickly that a slap rang out. Once again the queen turned to the boy. He tried very hard to keep the relief from his face as the stag struggled weakly beneath his hand, very much alive again.

"At least until now," the queen murmured before turning her heavy gaze back to their guest.

The man nodded, and the boy noticed he'd taken two steps back towards the door. "And many of us still support you, My Queen, but your attacks—"

"My self-defence," the queen corrected.

The man nodded again. "Your self-defence is hurting more than just your enemies."

The queen stood up, causing the man to back away until his shoulders thumped against the door. There was another jingle from the hallway as guards sprang back to attention.

"When my ancestors founded this kingdom," the queen began, and the boy lost track of what she said as once again the stag shifted beneath his fingers. A bent antler emerged from the pocket and sliced his skin creating a blossom of blood. The boy gasped and once again found himself under the heavy weight of the queen's attention.

"Apologies, my dear, but I'm feeling unwell," said the boy's stepfather by way of excuse, laying a cautioning hand on his son's shoulder. The queen sneered before turning back to their guest.

"As I was saying," she continued, stalking towards her prey who had nowhere else to go, "my family built all of this from nothing, and—"

Once more, the stag shifted within the boy's pocket. As he struggled against its movement and his stepfather's hand turned from a cautioning presence to a worried grip, he realized something. Before he could stop himself, he had turned to the queen and was speaking. "But our family did not build this kingdom," he exclaimed.

And suddenly the boy was back where he never wanted to be—at the centre of his mother's attention. The queen's icy eyes settled upon him, and in sheer panic, he continued.

"The city was founded by King Kelmir of the Bright Plain." He had never seen the queen so angry. "And before that, it was a ruin of a city founded by a religious order who worshipped the sun."

She was frozen in fury, but the boy found the words spilling out of him, too fast to stop. "And before that, it was a people who worshipped the volcano."

"There is no volcano," his stepfather interrupted, "so maybe let's—"

"Oh, but there was," the boy continued, "and there has been a tundra and a swamp and a star that fell and created farmland."

Finally, the nervous energy that kept him speaking ran out in the face of the queen's anger. The boy was empty, and the stag no longer struggled at his breast. His stepfather wrapped a shielding arm around him and said, "I suppose neither of us is feeling our best, my dear, so perhaps we should leave you two to your business."

Their guest did his best to melt into the rug and the door, but the queen remained imperious as she glared at the boy. Finally, she shifted her eyes to her husband. "What have you been telling him?" she demanded. She was a tall woman and had the voice of a giant—and the boy half expected the cording of her dress to snap as her chest heaved like a bellows.

"I have said nothing," his stepfather insisted.

"Then someone find me the person who has!"

The castle shook as everyone within earshot sprang into action, eager to prove their innocence by finding the guilty. The queen stormed from the room, scraping another groove into the doorframe with the sharp tip of her crown, and she no longer even noticed their guest. The poor man slid away from the door and bumped against a serving table sending serving spoons clattering to the stone floor.

"Stay out of sight," the boy's stepfather whispered, and then he ran off in pursuit of his wife, calling out platitudes that had ceased to work many years prior.

The guest and the boy looked at each other, and then the guest fled out into the hall and then into the castle grounds. The boy was alone, listening to chaos as the castle searched for someone who didn't exist. Finally, he reached into his top pocket for the troublesome stag, but all he found was a crushed, folded page marked with a small spot of blood. When he opened it, there was a stately woodcut of a white stag standing at the edge of a forest with a block of text about a long-ago battle.

"The White Stag of legend," the caption read, "said to have been born of a falling star."

And then the boy was off, shimmying through the castle walls and climbing up its interiors. He reached the second-floor linen closet and burst into the hall, causing a frantic maid to drop a neat stack of sheets. The boy ran towards his room. He heard the queen on the stairs, yelling at everyone she met and demanding to know what they knew. They sputtered senseless replies with quavering voices. Some blamed each other while others rightfully claimed innocence. His stepfather's voice trailed behind, but the old man's words were like birdsong to a storm.

The boy slammed his door and pulled the book out from beneath the cabinet. It didn't scratch or shift in his hands, but he pressed it to his chest and set off. First, he listened at the door, but the queen's voice was approaching, so he turned to the window and jumped to the ledge. As he sidestepped along in the cool morning air, the bedroom door burst open behind him.

"Search it all," came the queen's booming voice. "Find out who has been writing him."

Three windows later, the boy slipped into a guest bedroom with a thick, old carpet and a fireplace with a false back. From there he found himself downstairs in the throne room in a darkened corner where he stayed for several minutes while castle guards swept through looking for hidden traitors. Soon the boy climbed a post to a balcony with the large book under his arm. He slipped out a window and into a courtyard which contained a dried pond with a loose stone that opened between the walls of two rooms—one of which was the library.

There were muffled voices in the room beyond and the boy held his breath, just in case.

Two cleaners talked in hushed voices, but he could just make out their words.

"He's never been in here," said the first, an unknown man. "That boy couldn't sit still long enough to so much as read a cover."

The second was older with a deeper voice, and he recognized her as an upstairs maid. "If she lets him grow up, perhaps he'll be a better king."

"Let no one hear you say that."

"You don't think he'd be an improvement?" she asked incredulously.

"I'm not sure he'll get the chance, to be honest. We'd better lock this to be sure."

The boy listened a moment longer until he heard the click of the door, and then he pushed hard against the back of a shelf and entered the library.

In the distance, the queen's voice still echoed through the corridors, and the boy knew the next week of his life would be insufferable. His stepfather would try to make things seem normal, but the queen would be watching everything the boy did while the staff trailed him everywhere. It would be a long time before he'd return to the library.

He crept through the shelves and set the still book on the long study table. Curious numbers crept around his feet, more than were the last time. A seven tangled itself in the lace of his shoe and he had to shake it away. Then he took out the page that had been the white stag, and he flattened it to look at the woodcut once more. The other pages were back in place with no hint of life remaining, not even from the whale that had basked on the window sill. In the picture, the stag looked proud, its head raised and its dark eyes staring out at the reader. It was brave, strong, and clever, but just a picture in a book.

The boy wanted to carry that page with him forever, particularly in the tough week to come, but instead, he slid it back into the book in its original place where it failed to knit itself back into the spine.

The library doors rattled as a searcher attempted to enter and the boy froze solid, but they left when they found it locked.

"I'll tell my mother I remembered what I said from a lesson long ago," he whispered to the book, confiding in it as he would a friend. "It was a tutor who has left the kingdom and never returned, and I have forgotten all else she taught me." He tried to remember any of the tutors' names, but they disappeared so long ago that he couldn't. They were just a string of faces that bled together.

He picked the book up and held it to his chest once more, missing it before he'd even put it away. Now, it felt like any other book in his arms, and the boy's throat tightened and his eyes burned. Somehow it had gone dead, perhaps when he'd crushed the stag against his chest or when the information it contained released in the dining room. He couldn't be certain.

The queen's voice was getting louder, so the boy rushed to the shelf and pushed the travelogue back into its original place next to the strange swirling book. For a moment he watched that smaller book as it twisted, turned and rang in his head like a bell, but it eased itself further from the morning light. The queen was not far away, so the boy turned and ran, hoping to get into the castle walls before a key turned in the library door.

As he ran, he heard a sound behind him. It was a scratching sound, a noise from the books. As he raced through the shelves, they awakened around him. A book on herbology sent tendrils towards a distant window, and a book on sailing let out a salty breeze that stung the boy's eyes. As he entered the tunnel and pulled the shelf back into place to seal himself inside the walls, the boy got a glimpse of every book coming to life, and he had no idea why.

A key was turning in the lock of the doors. "Hide yourselves," the boy hissed, hoping that the books heard him and that no one else did.

He listened as the library was searched, but that was fine. They wouldn't find a tutor hiding away, and the searchers would then move on. It might be awhile before he could return, but as the boy caught his breath, he was smiling.

There was more reading to do.

Time Passes

nce upon a time, there was an older boy who lived in a castle that no longer seemed quite so large. It was not safe to leave the castle, so he knew its insides very well. He knew each stone of the tallest tower and each drain in the deepest dungeon. He knew which roof tiles loosened underfoot and which walls had hollows inside. As he'd grown, some of these secret ways became too snug to be useful, but he still moved through the castle free from the watchful eyes of the staff and, more importantly, the oppressive attention of his mother the queen.

His favourite place by far was the library—a long, cobwebbed room that stretched the northern wall on the second floor with its warren of shelves and soft, dusty chairs. Its grand double doors had been locked for years and hidden behind a wardrobe. That made it better because when the boy came in by one of his secret ways, he was alone with the books and didn't need to worry about servants or the queen, or even his tottering, old stepfather, who wandered the castle in a fog, never quite certain where he was or where he was going.

As soon as he could after breakfast, the boy squeezed into the castle walls to make his way to the library to read, which he didn't do in a conventional way. Instead, the books greeted the boy by unfolding before him until the library carpet was thick with paper-craft characters and places, battlefields and castles and kitchens. Each morning he sat in his dusty chair by the cold fireplace to have the contents of a book play out before him. That is how he learned.

The boy hadn't had a tutor since he was very young, but he had the books. They packed his head with knowledge the same way they swarmed the library with movement. He'd stay as long as he dared as they danced, pranced and fought around him, and then he'd settle everything back into their books and return to the rest of the castle to pretend to have a very mundane life.

His favourite characters had to be the stags. The library contained a thousand books, and the white stags came from two dozen or more, each with their own idiosyncrasies. From books on warcraft, the stags came bold and strong with their white coats marred by the grit of the battlefield, and these towered over the others at nine inches in height. From the romances, the stags came slim and subtle as unicorns, and their horns dripped ribbons and flowers. There was even one from a children's book, a tiny sketch of a beast, and it ran through the legs of its brothers with boundless energy, scraping their bellies with the nubs of its antlers.

His favourite stag was a simple flat page he'd tacked above the mantle which never moved at all. It was a wrinkled page though he'd pressed it as smooth as he could. This white stag stood proud and tall, staring out with a kindly confidence. Each day the boy checked it for the slightest hint of movement, but years passed without so much as a twitch of an ear.

When he wasn't in the library, the boy played at being a child. He stumbled about in front of the kitchen staff and fumbled in front of the knights. Most importantly, he played dumb as possible in the face of his mother the queen so she could smirk at his stupidity. At night, he retired to bed in a room full of his stepfather's toys he never touched, looking out the window to what remained of the village beyond.

Once, cannon fire hadn't bothered him. It had been as common as the tick of the clocks in the hall, but now he lay awake staring at the ceiling, listening to the booms that shook the glass of the window.

Now he'd seen battlefields. He'd watched paper-craft villagers slaughtered by men on horses and dragons, and so the village beyond the castle walls was more than a curiosity now. Once it had spread as far as the forest, and the sound of the villagers waking had been his morning crow, but most of the buildings had fallen or burned. Now a sea of tents spread towards the forest, filled with the low rumble of the queen's army.

Inside the castle walls, his stepfather grew more forgetful and the queen evermore grim, but otherwise most things stayed very much the same as the months and years passed by.

When he slept, the boy dreamt of the world but not the way it was. In his dreams, everything folded together and bore the strong, dark lines of a woodcut. People crinkled and scraped as they moved, and they spoke in the heightened language of books as they responded to commands of hidden authors. On troubled nights, when the screams at the castle gates left the boy unable to sleep, people in his dreams spoke to him in a troubling voice he'd once overheard many years ago as he listened to servants from inside the castle walls. "If she lets you grow up," they said, "perhaps you'll be a better king."

In the dreams, he ran from that, crashing through paper walls and falling through tissue floors. Sometimes lanterns tipped, and the world burned around him, leaving the boy to run through ash and fire.

On nights when there was neither sleep nor the crash of battle on the wind, the boy listened to the queen's steady footfalls as she paced the halls, and he'd stare into the darkness until morning.

The only person the boy could be himself with was his stepfather, and he allowed this for two reasons. First, the man was always kind to him. He'd married into the family when the boy was six, and he brought a great deal of money with him. Suddenly the castle walls were repaired and seven times as many knights stood in formation at the gates. More importantly, someone smiled at the boy, told him stories, and taught him games. The old man could not remember them now, so sometimes they would sit together and the boy would teach him in return, but everything was quickly forgotten again.

The boy couldn't remember much from before his stepfather came, but he remembered the old man teaching him how to play and encouraging the castle children to play with him. It had been a magical summer until the queen ended it all, accusing the boy of consorting with commoners. Still, his stepfather had guarded him and taught him when time permitted, shielding the boy from the worst of the queen, and for that and more, the boy loved him.

The second reason the boy was himself with his stepfather was the old man forgot everything he heard within the hour. It had started with little things, like forgetting to dress for dinner or losing track of glasses of milk all around the castle, but it had swiftly grown until the boy's own name disappeared from the old man's mind. Fortunately, he still knew his son, even if he couldn't name him—and the way you were certain was that his face softened whenever they met on the stairs or caught each other's eyes across the dinner table. Each time, the old man smiled proudly. The boy couldn't remember the father he was born to, but the old man had done what he could.

One day, after a fitful night of dreaming, the boy ran into his stepfather just before he slipped into the walls on his way to the library. The old man stood on a winding stair, trying to remember if he should go up or down, but his confused expression melted away when he saw his son coming towards him.

"Ah, a familiar face at last," the old man grinned.

"I have something I've meant to ask you," the boy said, sitting down upon a step. His stepfather lowered himself down on creaking knees, and their shoulders touched together.

The old man's memories of the past were much stronger than his grasp of the present, but he somehow he remembered to be careful with what he revealed to the boy for fear of possibly angering the queen. Family history was never a topic of conversation as the boy had more interest in life outside the castle. The boy's questions were about distant kingdoms and the way ships travelled against the wind, but lately, they'd turned towards the kingdom itself as the boy sought to understand the fighting and his own role within the family line.

There was very little recent history in the library. The boy always assumed the insurgency had reduced the urgency of expanding the library, but the old man's silence had begun to make the omission seem more surgical than circumstantial.

"I wanted to ask about my other father," the boy said. His stepfather's face became dark and clouded. The boy felt the avoidance building so he didn't give it the chance to take hold. "I know we've spoken about it so many times before," he blurted, and immediate the guilt crawled through his ribs.

The old man's brows knitted together. "Have we?" he asked so innocently that his son almost gave up the gambit.

"Several times and at great length," the boy replied. The boy leaned his shoulder more firmly against the old man's.

He'd been reading a book about tactics, which for him meant that paper people had played out scenarios before him. They were battlefield manoeuvers designed to trick the enemy and ways to gain the upper hand, deceits with armour and horses, hidden pits and diversions, but the boy came to see that the same techniques worked in many other contexts. He'd used it to get extra servings of pie in the kitchen and to ride a knight's horse around the yard, but he felt terrible about using the same tricks on the only person who loved him.

"Well, he was a good king," the old man began, "even though he didn't wear the crown for long. Your mother loved him dearly, and his loss changed her. I didn't meet her until years after, but she'd been known as the flower queen because of her love of the gardens. Your father filled them with flowers from the very edges of the world, and she delighted in watching things grow." The old man's voice faltered. "I supposed I fell in love with her from the stories," he finished.

The old man's face turned maudlin, and the boy wanted to head it off. He hoped dearly that any emotions being churned up would disappear with his stepfather's memory of this conversation, but he needed to press some more.

"And what of my siblings?" the boy asked, setting the question out as if it were a treat and not a trap laid in the dark. He stopped breathing as the old man smacked his lips.

"We shouldn't speak of the dead," the old man whispered, and the boy's mouth became suddenly dry.

He hadn't been certain, but there were other rooms in the towers, rooms with small beds and empty shelves. They may have been used centuries ago, but on one of the boy's explorations, he'd found a pair of shoes in an otherwise empty cupboard. They'd been quite new and so small.

"Oh, I know all about them," the boy lied once again, "I just like to hear about them so I don't forget."

His stepfather sighed deeply. "Three brothers you had, each one strong and smart as you and all before my time in the castle. The first was a jester, the funniest sort. The second, a poet with the heart of a dove. The third was a student, so seriously stern. Which leaves us, at last, with you."

The boy sat still, thinking of these three brothers he'd never known existed, all of them dead. One of them had once worn the shoes from the cupboard, and he wondered which it had been. Still, his mother's anger at the world clicked into place. Now the boy understood why this castle was his cage—because the world was not a kind place for princes.

The old man patted the boy's knee comfortingly. "When your father died in that ill-gotten storm on the sea and only your mother survived, she returned to the castle and locked herself in the north tower to mourn while you and your brothers waited for her to come down. When she finally did, she was very much changed, no longer the flower queen she'd once been. The world had been cruel, and so she decided to change it, and war has an effect on us all." The old man stared down at his hands. "Still, I think I sometimes see the woman she was."

The boy wasn't so certain, but he didn't interrupt. He grew up only seeing flowers in paintings. The gardens had crumbled into a wasteland, filled with broken siege weapons and a forge where sooty commoners made swords.

"When she finally recovered, she'd locked herself away so long that the boys barely recognized her, so she tried to make things right. She took the oldest on an ocean voyage so they might reacquaint, but the stormy seas stole him away as they had your father. She took the middle to the mountains so he might look down upon the world, but an icy slip resulted in tragedy. Finally, she took the younger to a city in the east, far from anything that could hurt him, but he caught an illness and wasted away before they returned."

The boy had to remind himself that these weren't his stepfather's sons, despite the sadness in the telling. The old man mourned the loss of these children deeply though their stories ended before he arrived.

"When she finally made it back, you had just begun walking. We met, and she built up the walls to keep everything out, and so you sit protected." The old man nudged his shoulder against his son's.

"You can't hold it against her that she kept you inside," he said. "Your brothers were a jester, a poet and a scholar. She doesn't know you're an explorer, in and out of the walls like a mouse through cheese."

The boy grew still again. "You haven't told her?" he asked delicately.

"Every child needs their secrets. I'm aware things aren't easy for you here, but don't judge her too harshly. She hasn't met you yet." The old man's cloudy eyes studied his son's face. "You don't meet your children when they're babes in blankets; they introduce themselves over months and years."

The old man sank into the sadness he spoke and the boy tumbled after, so he quickly changed the subject. He chattered away about the cinnamon bread at breakfast and the necessary repairs to the eastern wall until his stepfather's head spun with so much detail that his sadness faded. When the old man finally tottered off down the stairs, he did it with a lightened heart, unaware of the heavy thoughts he left churning behind him.

At dinner that night, the boy watched his mother with a new appreciation, and he wanted so much to ask more questions about his brothers, but the queen was in a funk due to a poor turn in the war. Hundreds of soldiers were cut off by a groundswell of peasants, and dozens of expensive horses were lost.

Instead, the boy stayed for dessert rather than slipping away and chatted quietly with his stepfather about the state of the pudding. He even played dumb when his mother made a mistake of geography and the old man struggled to remember the name of an epic poem the boy had watched play out only a week prior on the dusty library carpet.

If the queen wanted him safe within the castle walls, he could do that. She'd had more than enough loss for one life.

Discovered

The next morning when the boy slipped into the library and the books fluttered open before him, he called out for stories about curses. For the rest of the day, they showed him.

There were curses that destroyed beauty or finances and others that pulled down mountains and governments. There were curses that broke the mind and rendered men senseless and curses of death that stalked down family lines. Dark figures pursued paper maidens through chair legs and forests. Knights fought along the mantel and then fell to their deaths as curses stole away their strength. There was even a swarm of paper locusts that settled across everything so that the whole library shone green and the boy could not move. It took so long to shoo them back into their book that he missed seeing the sunset through the sliver in the curtains.

By the time he noticed, dinner had already begun. The boy ran through his passageways, into the third parlour and out into the halls, dodging past servants and sprinting down the main hall which still echoed behind him as he burst into the dining room.

The queen sat primly with her dinner untouched. Her maps were folded and her letters still sealed. His stepfather's face twisted with worry, and the boy looked for the slight shake that signalled to be quiet and invisible, but he realized it was far too late for that.

"And where have you been?" the queen murmured, which was more terrifying than any of her yelling.

"I fell asleep in my room," the boy replied quickly. He tried to look tired and raised a hand to stifle a yawn, but as he did, he noticed a cobweb trailing from his wrist. So too did the queen. It was a very large castle with many towers and rooms, but one thing it didn't have was cobwebs. The servants wouldn't allow them. They wouldn't dare.

"Your room seems to be in need of a tidy," the queen said icily.

The boy nodded, now noticing the dust on his knees. So too did the queen.

"And what part of napping leads to trousers like that?" she asked.

It was from the library carpet, the boy knew. Since sealing the library, no servants had entered, and the room had grown thick with dust. "I was also out in the stables," the boy replied, hoping the excuse would do but suspecting quite rightly it wouldn't. When the queen spoke this quietly, it didn't last, and the boy knew a storm approached—it was just a matter of when it would break. Sometimes she saved things up, leaving him to anticipate it for days.

"Your dinner is cold," she said simply, turning away, and a knot tightened in the boy's stomach. She tore at the edge of a letter with a butter knife and began to read.

This was to be one of those times. Perhaps he'd sleep in the dungeons or have his feather bed replaced with straw. She might take away his toys in the belief he used them since she didn't know her son very well at all. Most terrifying of all would be something new, leaving the boy not sure how to prepare.

His veins ran with cool dread as he took his seat at the table, and he tried to remind himself of the things he now knew. No matter what happened, she meant the best he told himself, repeating it over and over as she shuffled through her maps. He had no stomach for the food before him, but it seemed the only way to pass the time, so he kept his eyes down as the queen's paperwork spread across her end of the table. By the time the boy reached for his melted bowl of cream, his stepfather had forgotten anything was amiss and chatted quietly in his ear about naval history.

In fact, when a knock rang out at the hallway door, the boy thought he was through the worst of it. His heart even surged at the distraction, hoping that the interruption might draw the queen away or perhaps even cause her to forget his lateness entirely.

The butler was a severe older man constructed of corners and angles, and no matter how hard he tried, no livery disguised it. He stepped into the room and stood silently until the queen looked up from a scroll and turned towards him.

Several of the butler's joints popped as he bent into an awkward bow.

"Apologies for the interruption, Your Majesty," he said in a raspy voice.

The queen peered at him overtop her stack of pages, and to the butler's credit, he did not melt away.

"We've found something unusual in the third parlour," he continued.

The boy froze in place with a spoonful of cream halfway to his lips. The third parlour had been his way out of the walls as he'd dashed from the library towards dinner, and now, far too late, he realized he hadn't heard the click of the wall sealing tight behind him. He'd been in too much a rush to check.

"What has been found?" the queen asked, already turning towards the boy. He quickly set his spoon down and feigned curiosity.

The butler finally straightened from his bow with a few further pops. "There was an open panel in the wall with a passageway hidden behind," he replied.

The queen surged to her feet. "A secret passageway in the castle?" she demanded incredulously, and the boy's rising panic split into confusion. The queen had grown up here, and the passages riddled the castle. Surely she must have known of some of them.

"I fear so, Your Majesty," the butler replied.

"Find out where it goes," she spat.

"But someone may be in the castle, Your Majesty."

The queen shook her head, not looking away from the boy. "There's no one in the castle." She paused for a moment, and the boy thought this might have been the first time she really looked at him in a very long time. "And look for others—seal them up as well."

The boy didn't hear the butler leave. The next thing he knew the queen stood beside him, looking him straight in the eye as the surrounding castle sprang to life carrying out the queen's orders.

"I believe I have left you on your own for too long," the queen said calmly and ever so sweet. It left the boy feeling deeply unseated, as if the world now spun the wrong way around. "There's so much more of the world to see," she continued. "This kingdom will someday be yours, my son, and so this is what I propose." The queen placed a pale, cool hand on his.

"In a week's time, the army should be back at home." She'd never spoken like this before, and he didn't recognize it at first as he sat frozen in place. His mouth moved to form words that didn't come out, and the queen smiled. It was an awkward smile of someone who'd once seen one or read about them in a book—and suddenly he recognized her tone.

In the library, he'd seen civilizations rise and fall, listened to all manner of stories, and in many of them, there were families who loved each other and wished each other well from the start. In some of those, paper-craft mothers hugged their children tightly and spoke words of comfort and caring, and the boy spent long afternoons wondering if those sorts of families were common or if they were relics of a distant past.

The queen parroted those sentiments as well as she could, but it fell far short of sincerity as she leaned even closer and squeezed his hand. "Yes," she said finally, "I think it's time we went on a trip."

Then she turned away and stalked out of the room, off into the castle at large where already servants called out as they discovered his warren of tunnels, the ladders, and hollows that let him move about.

Beside him, the boy's stepfather let out a laugh. "That sounds like jolly good fun," he said. To the old man, it did. The boy, however, thought of three other trips with three other sons, realizing they no longer sounded as innocent as they had before.

As he walked back to his room, the boy saw servants testing tiles and knights knocking on walls. The butler rolled up a carpet under the queen's observation, and others peeked behind tapestries. The queen's eyes followed the boy as he climbed up the grand central staircase which felt so foreign underfoot after so many years in the walls. When the boy got to his room, he found a maid nailing the window shut while a knight mortared down the loose corner tile.

Escape

The castle groaned with construction for the next three days, and at dinner each night, the queen updated the boy on the progress of the army. "They've now cleared the northern hills so they're just three days away," she said sweetly, but her eyes were far colder than before. "Soon we can leave on our journey."

It wouldn't make things better, but the boy couldn't help himself. "This time of year, the Elliel River runs deeper, so it will be two further days of diversion," he replied.

The feigned sweetness drained from the queen's face. She spoke no more to him that day.

Now the boy wore the butler like a shadow, and every moment he was out of his room, the man walked just ten steps behind. So too the castle staff and the knights in the yard turned their heads whenever the boy passed as they studied this child who was so suddenly interesting—no longer a simple nuisance underfoot, but now a boy of secrets.

When the construction finally quieted again, the boy saw signs of the changes everywhere. The dining room panel no longer whistled when the wind picked up, various tiles had bright new grout around them, and the relocated furniture only made sense when you knew what was now locked away behind.

Woodcuts

He felt more constricted than ever. He thought of escape constantly, but he had no idea which routes remained open to him or thought of where he'd go if he did. Additionally, the prince believed he'd only get one chance. At night, the queen was no longer the only one who paced the halls, and the first two nights he hardly slept due to the butler's snoring outside his door.

The boy was lonely, despite almost never being alone. His stepfather still chattered away about ships, oblivious to the surrounding changes, but the boy missed the library and the books. He missed the clatter of stag hooves upon the fireplace tile and the elusive authors peeking out from between pages. He even longed for the strange swirling book that rang like a bell in his head, which he had decided was the power of the library, though he still couldn't tell why.

His thoughts returned to the books, including the first two that had awoken. One was just full of numbers, which still didn't interest him. The other contained history, the rise and fall of kingdoms, and a white stag who had been his closest friend once before an accident had turned it back into a simple woodcut. The boy also wasn't sure why the magic had spread, eventually affecting every book in the room, but he somehow felt responsible. It had happened during a tense moment as the boy fled from the queen, and he maintained there was a connection.

As the boy thought of his favourite dusty chair and the picture of the stag pinned above the fire, he sat bolt upright in bed. For the first time in days, he smiled. He dug through a trunk of unloved toys as quietly as possible so as to not awaken the butler sleeping on the hard floor of the hall. It was all he could do not to crow when he found what he sought—a drawing buried beneath childish trash, one he'd made after finding the first books.

It wasn't good. The stag had jagged antlers, and the poor beast looked more like a sickly dog than the stately stag of legend, but it was all he had. He dug more and found the box of charcoals he'd used to draw it, and he flipped the page over and wrote a short message.

By the time he ventured down to breakfast, the rolled-up page was secreted inside his sleeve, and he hurried through eating while the kitchen staff eyed him warily. They'd discovered his tunnel that ran behind the kitchen wall along with so many of the others, so now they were even more suspicious of him than they'd ever been before. No one knew what he'd overheard or what he'd repeated. They lived in worry that their sour words were being passed back to the queen, so they stayed well away, except for the butler who had no choice but to follow along.

That day, the butler trailed the boy around the castle grounds, through the tangle and smithy that had been the queen's prized garden, past the stables and around the outer walls. He watched the boy pick through the apples in the

orchard in search of just the right one, and when the butler
returned after a quick nip to the garderobe, the boy still sat on a
lower branch, kicking his feet in the cool, fall breeze.

At dinner, the queen had difficulty focussing on her
maps and letters and kept glowering at the boy. There was
something different about him she just couldn't place, though
he pushed his food around his plate and chatted quietly with his
stepfather in his usual way.

"The army is just a few days away," she said, exploring.

The boy turned to the queen and smiled just slightly.

"I thought we might go to the seaside," she continued.

"If you like," he replied, and then he turned back to his
stepfather to whisper about the weather.

That seemed to satisfy her, and she returned to her
letters.

They were still getting accustomed to the quiet that
followed the recent construction. At first, the boy thought
nothing of the slightest noise at the window, a tapping that
came and then went. He thought of the library and wondered
about the drawing he'd left at the window, but he wasn't certain
if the magic would work or how long it might take. When the
main course finished, they awaited dessert. The boy heard the
sound again—a tapping at the window so soft that only young
ears could hear it over the rustling of maps and the tearing of
envelopes. He almost ignored it, but then he saw a flicker of
white from the corner of his eye.

The antlers were wrong, and the stag shook like an excitable terrier, but it tapped its head excitedly against the glass and the boy almost leapt towards it. Instead, he bit his lip and looked at the carrots on his plate.

"Could I be excused?" the boy asked quietly.

His stepfather stalled halfway through a story he'd told a hundred times before about the fleet of ships he'd once owned, sputtering to a stop with concern. The queen merely nodded as she shuffled through her papers, and the boy set off for his room.

The butler approached in the hallway carrying a silver tray of puddings, and he nearly dropped the lot as the boy burst past him. As the boy arrived in the main hall, he saw the misshapen stag squeeze itself under the doors and gallop towards him on uneven legs. He scooped it up and sped up the stairs, listening as a footman tried to catch up and trying to keep the stag from licking his chin. Halfway up the stairs, he paused, now aware of another sound. He pressed his ear to the wall, and listened to the scratching and tapping within, and the footman almost caught up before the boy set off again with a wide grin upon his face.

When he reached his room, he turned on the footman who had just rounded the corner behind him. "I'm just turning in early," the boy said, lightly cupping the stag in his hands. It wagged its tail which made its whole body wiggle, and it was all the boy could do to keep his hands still. The footman stopped and straightened his liveries, trying not to pant as the boy disappeared into his room and shut the door quickly behind him.

Paper-craft people crowded the floor. There were workers who he'd watched build cities and bridges loosening the tile in the corner. There were tiny bellhops and labourers loading the boy's things onto the backs of horses and elephants, griffins and dragons, and a whale was enjoying the moonlight on the window sill. The boy set down his stag on the bedroom floor where other stags crowded around it, nosing at it as it rolled over for someone to scratch its belly and getting its antlers caught up in the rug.

There were also the thieves, spies and cutthroats, and they gathered close around the boy and laid out a table of contents, across which someone had drawn the plans for the castle, carefully marked with every room and passage, including some the boy had never found for himself.

A knight stepped forward, using a spear to plot their course. "So, this is how we get you out, Your Highness. There's a work crew reopening this passageway and that, as well as a ladder to the dungeons. Diggers are extending the tunnel and by dawn it should reach beyond the castle walls."

The boy looked at the plan with a smile on his face but then shook his head. There were figures in the fireplace, scraping up soot to darken the prince's face for a nighttime escape. Villagers swarmed across the bed, building a likeness of the prince beneath the blankets. Already many of his belongings disappeared into the floor in the corner, but they didn't take the toys. They didn't think to, because these books knew him and understood what he'd want to bring—with one notable exception.

"There's one more stop along the way," the prince said, reaching down to take the spear and to redraw their path for the night.

And so it was that the boy left the castle hours before dawn through a tunnel beneath the wall, carrying as many empty books as he could handle and nothing else. At the top of his pile, a book swirled and rang in his head like a bell.

He paused for a moment. In the darkness, he realized that for the first time in his life there were no castle walls around him. It felt like the wind might carry him away, but then barking of a lopsided stag that tugged at his shoelaces brought him back to himself. Around them swarmed paper beasts and people carrying leather covers and spines upon their backs and in talons and paws. They disappeared into the long grass of the fields with the castle at their backs.

With one last look at the castle behind them in the fading light of day, the prince set out on a journey.

The Kingdom

nce, there was a young man in a very large world. His home consisted of stone and wood, deep within a dark forest and hidden far from the closest path. It was round and squat, nestled under the boughs of evergreens taller than a castle tower, and as you approached the cottage, you heard a rustling inside like a restless colony of bats.

The home was cozy, and just enough for the young man and the thousand books that lived with him. As he walked from bed to desk, he ducked beneath a flock of paper geese and stepped over the oldest man, who stood just four inches tall but trailed an endless paper beard. Some friendlier books murmured as the young man passed, and he patted them as he did. They were his friends, and he'd listened to every one of their stories. He'd grown up with them in the castle library, and he'd brought them all with him when he ran—every book in the castle but one.

There were books on history and science, books on irrigation and engineering, books of romance and adventure too. There was also one book of magic, a slim book that hid away between the others but rang in the young man's head like a bell whenever he got too close.

The house had taken three weeks to build and had stood tall for a year, but the young man hadn't built it alone. Each of the books had helped in their own way, sending out their pages in the form of the woodcuts and drawings they contained. Small labourers emerged from books on construction and hewed the posts for the cottage walls. Tiny miners cut into the mountain for stone. Even the numbers tried to help, wedging things in place while the mortar dried or forming the bones of the scaffolds.

When the build began, kings and architects oversaw the work, but a turn in the weather made the situation dire for the paper workers. The prince spent two desperate days trying to keep everyone dry in the skeleton of the cottage they'd built. Finally, when all hope was lost, the authors emerged, climbing from their books like spirits and guiding their creations to create. The characters and drawings were clever in their own ways, but they were only mimics of what they represented, limited by the manner in which they were written. The authors though, or at least the good ones, had put all of themselves into their writing.

A general climbed out of a book of tactics, and he organized the woodcuts into order, prioritizing the roof to defeat the rain. An elf from the pages of the travelogue oversaw the weaving of leaves into shingles and the coaxing of glass from sand without the use of heat that kept the harshest winds at bay. The young man had watched it done and still didn't understand the process. There was also a librarian from a book of poetry who nursed the soggy books back into shape so they were firm and strong again, and under her careful care, few covers were lost to rot or pages swollen and torn.

When the house was complete, the authors faded back into their books like a memory, and the young man settled into a quiet life of living off the land and staying unnoticed.

People still came. Sometimes they stumbled through the forest and the paper sentries signalled back long before they reached the house. Then the young man covered the windows and blocked the door, disguising the cottage so carefully that strangers trailed their fingers along its side and still didn't know it was there.

Sometimes these were the queen's men, searching far and wide for their prince to drag him back to the castle. Sometimes these were villagers, lost and hiding, trying to find a new way to a neighbouring kingdom where they might, at last, be safe, and these the prince wanted to meet. They were the ones he'd so often seen shouting at the castle gates or dragged before the queen's version of justice, but the tiny paper advisors and tacticians around him would not let him go. The queen was clever and anyone passing by was suspect to their eyes. Instead, the young man sent out dragons and stags and small parchment wishes, and these subtly led the people away while the prince watched from a distance.

He hoped they travelled to safety, but based on the news of the scouts who ventured out each morning, he wasn't certain such a thing existed.

Years passed in this way, with the occasional boom of a cannon in the distance or a scream in the night, always followed by cautioning voices that gathered near the prince's ear in the darkness. But there were other books as well—books of adventure and daring, books of pirates and fighting, and these characters also sought the prince's ear, whispering to the youth of freedom. There were thieves and travellers, merchants and rangers, and many disappeared to scout the forest, returning within three days before their magic ran dry. They carried back salvaged pottery and food for the table, word of empty villages and descriptions of slaughter in the field.

This was how the prince found out about the tide of the war and the darkening of the land, the empty villages and the queen's growing solitude, surrounded by her murderous army. There was never news of his stepfather, and the prince spent wakeful nights wondering about the old man's fate and wishing he had brought him on his escape. There hadn't been time, and the prince felt a tightness in his chest because he also wasn't certain the old man would have come.

Eventually, the prince grew too curious, and one day he slipped away from the cottage with two books strapped to his back and a single stag in his top pocket wagging its tail and yipping like a dog. The first book was the travelogue that had awoken first, full of beasts and civilizations stretching back thousands of years or more, as well as the elven author whose spirit hid within.

The second was the slim book of magic that rang in his head like a bell. Try as he might, even after years with it, the book made no more sense than it had the very first day. There were moments when the prince swore letters appeared within the swirling ink, but then the headaches came. When the youth grew strong enough to open his eyes again, days had passed and the book was no less of a mystery.

As the prince quietly locked the door behind him, he didn't look back, knowing if he saw just one drawing at the window, he might never see the kingdom. He walked for some time before unstrapping the travelogue and holding it open, and all manner of winged creatures burst forth and took to the sky to lead him on.

The first night, the prince settled in the ghost of a barn. Its bones rose into the night sky like burnt ribs. The stars shone down as he settled into sleep with tiny knights patrolling the perimeter and a griffin monitoring the sky. The dog-like stag yipped through the grass, chasing off crickets and mice.

By day, they walked. The fields grew tall with weeds and thistle, and scouts kept having to scamper back through the grass to turn the prince in a new direction before he could smell the sickly scent of death. Sometimes they weren't quick enough, and the prince saw more bones than a butcher in his first day of walking, but he saw no signs of life—just village after village of cinder and decay.

The second night, the prince made his bed in a shed by a well. An engineer warned him against the water which was fouled with poison. The woodcuts played for the prince to distract him from the sights that haunted his thoughts, showing him the rise and fall of a wizard's tower cursed by a demon of the swamp. The youth had seen this story countless time and had always loved seeing the demon's hand rise up from the fetid water to pull the tower down, but that night, it couldn't distract him from the wind in the fields and each rustle of grass.

The prince slept very little. He missed the comfort of the castle walls that had held the world at bay, as well as the simple pleasure of hiding in the walls where the world couldn't find him. That morning they turned back, taking a different path through a forest. By the third night, they took refuge in the ruins of a manor house in the remains of a small village, just hours away from where the cottage lay hidden.

"How could there be no one left?" the prince asked the stag as it rolled about on his belly, chasing after a length of grass he dangled there. The house was dark, save for the gentle swirling glow of the magic book tied to the prince's gear and not able to hide away.

The house was the only part of this village still standing since it was the only one built of stone, but the queen's fire had taken the roof and crumbled several walls. They were in the most intact room remaining, which had once been a study. Its beautiful marble fireplace had cracked, and the shelves had fallen. Little rain got in, and so it stayed dry while offering shelter from the wind.

The stag looked the young man in the eyes and cocked its head, unbalanced by its awkward antlers, but it did not answer. The prince had drawn this stag himself, and most of its charcoal shape had long since smudged away. It had none of the wisdom of the others, though even theirs seemed like a shadow of something else, a greater truth the prince couldn't understand. What this stag knew was freedom and play, the joy of wind in its antlers and the chase offered by a long piece of grass. Eventually, it settled in the crook of the prince's arm and he ignored the sharp poke of its antlers against his skin.

On their walk, they had seen no sign of life beyond the tracks of a mounted battalion along the road. The prince's dreams were of a dead world stretching from one ocean to the next being picked over by rats and crows until they too starved away. In the dreams, he was the last one alive—just him and the books which in turn crumbled away, leaving the prince entirely alone. When he suddenly woke, the sound of the queen's pacing echoed in his ears, but the manor house itself was silent.

Or almost silent.

The prince had become so used to the sound of surrounding books that it had ceased to be a sound at all. They were there, guarding his sleep and gathering around the pale light of their illustrated fires to take comfort in the night. A general took notice of the prince and called out that all was quiet and the prince nodded in response, but the dog-stag stood alert in his arms, staring into the darkness of the fireplace.

There was another sound in the room, a shifting of wood and stone, and now the prince was up and on his guard. He snatched up the book that rang like a bell in his head and opened the cover wide, casting its pale pink light around like a beacon. Everywhere, his paper guards sprang to their feet and readied their weapons.

The pale light of the book did little to illuminate the jagged shapes of the desk and the ruined shelves around them, but the stag had begun a low growl, and various other creatures crept outward to investigate. It was probably rats or squirrels, but the prince wasn't ready to be certain, so he let out a quick whistle into the night.

Above, a dragon from a poem about beauty settled on an exposed rafter. It let out a puff of fire that filled the room with light, and the prince saw his knights gathering at the window and his beasts creeping out from beneath the tattered sofa, their eyes catching in the firelight. But there was another movement too, and as the dragon released a second puff, the prince saw small figures pulling themselves from the manor house debris.

They stood torn and smudged. Many had burns around their edges. Some desperately tried to hold themselves together where they'd split, but they came anyway from beneath the ash and the bricks, the kindling of the bookshelves and the yellow bones of men. The books of the manor house gathered in the dragon's light and looked up at the prince who bathed in the pink glow of his swirling magic book.

"Hello," he breathed.

This house's library was smaller than the castle's had been and most of the books were destroyed beyond usefulness, but the prince recognized several woodcuts before him because he'd met their doubles. There was a white stag from a book on forestry standing with one antler sheared away and a healer from a book on poultices and bandages leaning on a crutch made of a sliver of a shelf, but there were also new figures. There was a house that walked on chicken legs, and an empress dressed all in brown who sparkled in the dragon fire. There were yellow ducks in a series and a cluster of serious people in dark robes who kept to the shadows.

The prince moved to introduce himself when he spotted something else in the darkness of a corner, the slightest movement that drew his eye. He shifted the book to cast its light upon it and signalled to the dragon to adjust its fire.

First there came a man in a purple tunic and emerald leggings with a crown upon his head stepping out from behind a coal scuttle, and he raised a hand against the dragon's glare. He then reached back to help three sons climb into the light, each smaller than the last. The tallest swung his legs over a brick before reaching back to help a brother climb after. The second watched in awe as the dragon took flight. The third stepped carefully as his father held his hand, cataloguing the sight before him while clutching a book to his chest.

Finally, there followed a small woman in a violet gown with her hair braided and twined around her head and topped with a golden circlet. She struggled up last with her husband's help because she carried a baby in her arms, wrapped up tight against the chill of the evening.

The prince blinked once and then twice. He caught the magic book as it tried to slip from his hands. By the time he turned the glow back towards the family, they'd sat upon the brick, huddled together against the cold, and the baby fussed and began to cry.

The prince had seen his father in a painting hung along the castle stairs though he'd never seen his brothers before. They looked just as his stepfather had described and so the prince knew them all at once. One playfully threw ash at his brothers while the third barely looked up from the book in his hands. The second stared around in wonder at the ruins of the room and watched with wide eyes as the dragon swooped low overhead.

And then there was his mother. As the prince knelt down before them, she looked up and smiled sweetly, and he did not recognize her. No portrait of her in her youth hung inside the castle walls, and no one had explained how small she had seemed or how straightly she stood. There'd been no mention of the graceful way she tilted her head or the gentleness with which she held her child. This delicate woman who smiled so nervously was a stranger to him, a woman not yet broken by the grief of the world.

And then, of course, the prince looked down at himself, mewling in a knot of blankets in the queen's gentle arms. The baby was only a few scrapes of the pencil with slits for eyes and an O-shaped mouth that yawned as the child shifted and drifted back to sleep.

"Hello," the prince said again quietly. He touched the tip of a finger against the baby's cheek, which felt like soft, warm flesh and cool, rough paper—and both were true together. "That's me," he whispered.

His father beamed up at him, and tears formed in his mother's eyes. His brothers gathered close, and soon the trickster climbed up his arm to throw sticks for the dog-like stag, and the poet stared into the prince's eyes with a deep, meaningful stare.

This wasn't his real family, of course. For the rest of the night, the boy spoke with them, but it was an author's voice he heard, a man who came to court for a summer and wrote about it in a journal while drawing sketches in the margins. Their knowledge was bounded by their writing, and the prince often found himself against its edges with his father at a loss for words.

The prince's eldest brother appeared like a blur because the boy never sat still. The king doted on his wife and children and spoke boldly of his plans for the future, explaining alliances and his plans for a bridge to the islands. The queen remained uncharacteristically shy, but by dawn, she spoke of her gardens, the stories her father told when she was very young and he was well, and the seeds he brought back from far-off lands which he watched flourish under her capable hands from his sick bed in the castle library.

As her sons explored the manor ruins with their father and the dog-like stag in the morning light and the baby suckled, the queen spoke of her hopes for her children. One would be king, of course, but all would be happy, and it was just as simple as that.

Still, the prince noticed her watching him when she thought his attention was elsewhere, and there was a sadness growing in her voice. He did his best not to talk about the present, but his tunic showed signs of wear and a tear at the seam and their surroundings were far less than opulent. She soon called her boys back and held them close to her side.

The prince remained rapt, held captive by every word, breathing in this family that almost was. The author had clearly adored his time with them because he wrote them with such a lovely pen, and the prince believed them entirely. When the sun finally burned the fog away, everyone left the manor house and took what remained of this small library with them, trailed by the more intact pages that carried each other. In his top pocket, his family peered out at the journey, telling stories about stately dinners and balls that overflowed the same large, old ballroom the prince remembered merely as a secret way into the kitchens.

"Ah, yes," his father said cheerfully, "I've used that one myself."

"Your father is forever in and out of the walls," his mother laughed, and the prince delighted in the love between them. They walked on for a while longer before the prince stopped at the edge of the forest he called home and looked down at the family in his pocket. An idea itched at the prince, and he lost track of the conversation.

"So you knew about the passageways?" he asked finally, trying to keep his voice steady. "Not just your author, but you, the queen?"

"Of course," his mother replied with a look of concern, and she held the baby just a bit closer. "I even added a few of my own."

The itch only grew more distracting as they entered the forest along the hidden paths. He hardly noticed how sluggish the books he'd left behind had grown in his absence or heard the rebukes of the advisors who'd cautioned him to stay. His safety, they said—his duty to the crown to survive. The dangers if the queen had found him, or perhaps worse, the populace with whom the crown made war. A din of arguments filled the crowded cottage, now further packed by several more books than its design allowed.

But the prince couldn't hear it because his thoughts screamed much louder. He remembered the surprise in the old queen's voice when the butler found the secret door and her growing fury as they found each additional path. The castle was riddled with tunnels and hidden stairs, ladders and loose panels. Somehow, they'd remained hidden from the castle staff, but they'd opened to the prince like a birthright, and so they should have once opened for the queen. It was either something she'd forgotten or something she'd never known—or perhaps something she didn't wish to admit.

Around him, the cottage shifted from admonitions to welcomes as the new pages and books joined into the fold. All afternoon, the woodcuts sewed spines and replaced covers, glued pages back together and ironed creases away. By dinnertime, the new arrivals were in order and the spirits of the authors gathered around the table to plan an extension for the new books.

The prince looked down at the meal the cookbooks had provided and thanked them for the work they'd done. Then he stood up and looked around the room, knocking his head against a drawing of a cloud drifting past.

"Tomorrow we start preparations," the prince said loudly as every head turned towards him. "We have someplace we need to go, and we will all go there together." All around the cottage, faces gaped at the prince both human and beast, and he smiled in return. The young prince bubbled with the thrill of finally, after all this time, having an idea, and he laid out the journey and listened to the wisdom of the room as to how it should happen. They would find the people, he told them, however many of them remained, and within minutes, his advisors walked across unfolding maps and atlases, arguing over geography and precedents.

Eventually, the prince drifted to sleep listening to hushed voices still deep in planning.

Subjects

The next day, the prince woke with the sun. The elven author again directed as leaves were woven together into protective covers for the books. Engineers drew up plans for carts that could travel rough terrain and harnesses for tiny elephants and whales who swam through the sky—any manner of beasts capable of pulling or carrying. Within a week, they left the forest behind and walked out into the bright plains in a long narrow line, covering their tracks as they did to confuse any who might follow.

The journey took nine days, and throughout, countless pages took to the sky in search of signs of life, whether it be the slimmest trail of a campfire or the wide smudge of a surviving village or military encampment. They passed hamlets and villages, towns and farmlands, while skirting widely around the queen's forces. Finally, a griffin wheeled back to the long line of books so its rider could report a thin line of smoke from the centre of a deep, dark wood.

They approached with caution, hiding the bulk of their contingent in the long grasses at the forest's edge, and the drawings argued vehemently with the prince when he announced his intention to proceed alone. He had to command the books to remain behind, recruiting a contingent of knights to make certain no one followed him into the forest. He did not want to risk terrifying anyone with the magical creatures when they must already be in fear for their lives.

Finally, the prince stepped into the treeline on shaking knees with just two books strapped to his back—the travelogue and the book that rang in his head like a bell. In his top pocket, his family was tucked away out of sight along with the dog-like stag that yipped at every snapped twig, but it was quickly silenced by a firm command from the king. From the pocket, the prince's family listened to the frantic beating of his heart as he inched his way into the woods. The paths were carefully hidden, but not carefully enough to fool a prince who'd learned to track from heroes of legend on the dusty expanse of a library carpet.

He almost sighed in relief when he heard a branch crack and saw two large men step into the light. "I mean you no harm," the prince said with a deep bow. It was a simple truth because he was a bedraggled youth with no shoes who wore a torn tunic and carried nothing but books on his back.

They tied his arms and knotted a blindfold tightly over his eyes, still sniggering to each other about the prince's bow. For a long time, they pushed and nudged the youth along a twisting path which sometimes forced them to climb over fallen trees or crawl down beneath them. At times he was certain they took him in circles. If he hadn't seen the map the griffin rider drew of the forest and the location of the campfire, the prince would have been entirely lost. Finally, they shoved him forward, tore the cloth from his eyes and he saw his countrymen, such as they were.

They were a tired lot and far fewer than he'd hoped. About twenty people gathered among the trees, and the prince stood beside the tiny cookfire that served them all. Haggard and thin, many still nursed wounds and at least two had arms that stopped at the elbow. More than one rested a hand on the hilt of a weapon as if this slip of a lad might prove their undoing. The trees here were dense, and no sun reached the forest floor.

The prince chose not to introduce himself immediately. Instead he searched their faces, hoping to find clues about their feelings for the crown. He was not optimistic after so many years under the thumb of the queen. Similarly, he found himself uncertain as to how to begin, as his conversations had always been with servants to the crown or paper figures who often spoke in the poetic language of writers. The prince was trying to remember the counsel of his tacticians when an older woman stepped forward. She dressed in rags with her grey hair tied back, and her eyes twinkled with cleverness in the firelight.

"My prince," she said, curtseying as low as her old legs would allow, "we've been looking for you."

All at once, the clearing fell silent. The prince felt a glimmer of hope and saw that same glimmer reflected in many faces around him. He let go a breath he hadn't realized he was holding.

"I came to help," he said quietly.

"We'd given up," the woman replied, and she took half a step forward to embrace him before stopping uncertainly. The prince realized he'd taken a step back, but there was something familiar about the old woman that the prince could not shake, something in the way she lowered herself down by the fire and held her shoulders back. Perhaps it was the way she looked at him as if he had finally come home again.

"I've had to hide," the prince said carefully, stepping towards a circle of elders around the fire and sitting beside them. "I wasn't certain I'd be welcome."

The old woman smiled, and everyone clustered close around to listen as they spoke. "We heard you escaped from the castle," she said, "and we've seen the way the queen's forces still scour the kingdom to find you these many years later. We thought you'd gone to far-off lands to start your life anew, but to see you here will be a rallying cry, a call to all survivors." She patted his knee kindly, and that seemed familiar too. He never saw anyone touch his mother the queen, and the prince wondered if touching royalty was even permitted for a commoner.

An older man shook his head, tossing more sticks to the flames. "There's not enough left to rally, my friend. We should still make for the border. Already the neighbouring lands prepare to sweep through this cursed place and take it away from the princeling's family." He wiped his mouth with the back of a hand and then took a swig from a bottle. "We cannot defeat the queen's forces but it won't stop others from trying and crushing everyone beneath their armies as they go."

"Perhaps," the woman replied, but she really paid the old man no mind. Her attention remained on the prince alone. "You must eat, Highness. Eat and tell us where you've been and what you've been doing. Tell us of the others and give us hope."

The prince was hungry and ashamed of it in their presence. Their cook pot sat beside the fire half full of the thinnest of soups, and it was far too little for this many mouths.

"In hiding," the prince replied, his face reddening as he tried to sit tall before them. For the last few years, the books had sheltered him, keeping him dry and fed. He had servants and hunters and soldiers, though none of them real, and had lived like a king while these people went wanting. The prince grew up with their suffering in his ears, with the blasts of the cannons and the screams at the gates. He ate his desserts while his mother plotted their deaths and spent long afternoons in the library learning poems and songs while they bled in the fields for their freedom. It had just been so normal, like breathing, because they somehow hadn't felt real enough.

And now they crowded around him to listen, wounded and broken. They were already realizing that this ragged prince had no army of his own and could offer them no hope, and men muttered amongst the trees.

The prince tried to think of anything other than their stink. It was so strong he thought he might retch.

"Don't cry, my prince," the woman said kindly, and it was only then that he realized that he was. She patted his cheeks with a soiled bit of rag, and the prince had to fight the need to pull away. "Your brothers cried when I was dismissed," she continued, "sent from the castle in the night by your mother the queen, and you just a babe barely walking."

He looked at her again but still could not name her. The tutors bled together in his mind, tall and boring, and this one had known his brothers. She'd left well before his memories began, and yet there was something about her.

"I taught your brothers to read, each one," she said, sitting back and poking at the fire with a branch, "and I would have taught you if I wasn't dismissed. When your mother came home having lost the king, everything became different. She immediately locked herself away and let the garden die. The mistress of the keys took care of your brothers, but then she too was sent away." The woman's face grew shadowed as she spoke, and the prince knew she was a monarchist down to the core. No matter what became of the kingdom, to this woman royalty remained something to respect despite everything she had seen.

"Your mother had almost been my friend," she said carefully, "as much as a queen could be to a tutor, but grief drove her mad in the tower. We heard her screams in the night as it transformed her into whatever it is she is now. It was almost a relief when she sent me away—just a guard at my doorway in the middle of the night, and your brothers screaming from a window."

She dipped her head to apologize to the prince for saying unkind things about the crown, but they were true, and as far as the prince was concerned, there were far worse things to say.

"I would have stayed for you and your brothers," she said firmly. "I would have stayed until the castle burned around us, but I think your mother knew I wasn't strong enough for what she was planning, so she didn't even say goodbye."

The paper princes began to climb in the true prince's top pocket, squirming towards the familiar voice, but the prince held them back.

"The queen is as mad as you say," he said softly, letting the tutor see he felt no slight. "She intended to kill me and I fled."

A murmur spread around the clearing, passed around by lips that would not kiss a ring and speakers who would no longer bow. "So that's why you did it," the older man said, exchanging a dark look with several of the others.

The tutor shushed the man and pushed a small bowl of the watery soup into the prince's hands. "We cannot judge him or what he did. He was a child in captivity with no one to guide him."

At that, the books on the prince's back shuffled in their harness, and he momentarily released his grip on his pocket.

One of his brothers struggled free before getting trapped between the prince's fingers, but as the paper poet was caught, the dog-stag tumbled free and landed in the dead leaves of the clearing with soup spilling down around him.

People jumped back as the stag barked and then bounded over twigs and leaves towards the fire, wagging its tail gleefully at the company. It danced around the ring of stones before flopping over on its side at the prince's feet, waiting for a scratch of its belly.

"What is that?" the older man demanded. He sprang to his feet and held aloft a burning branch he threatened to swipe at the stag, but the prince snatched the drawing up into the safety of his hands.

"It's just a drawing," the prince blurted, "a bit of magic woven into paper."

He looked around beseechingly at the terrified gathering and then looked back at the tutor for support.

But she wasn't looking at him, not quite. Her eyes grew wide and her face aglow, and she leaned forward with dreamlike slowness. She looked at his top pocket and his brothers there waving. Behind them stood the king, gathering his children carefully against his chest and eyeing the burning branch before them.

"And that's them to a T," the tutor said with a breath. She motioned for calm and then raised a hand to the prince's pocket and the brothers spilled forth. They remembered this tutor, so much so that he wondered if she'd been a character in the book before it had been ruined in the destruction of the manor. They frolicked across her hand and climbed up her arm, and her face shone brightly as she watched them. The poet whispered into her ear, the trickster pulled at her hair, and the scholar sat on her sleeve with his book.

"It's as if they were right here before me," she laughed, lit from within by her wonder. She looked from brother to brother and then smiled at their father who assisted the queen as she climbed up onto the prince's shoulder.

The clearing grew chilly, and the prince sensed the gathering grow yet colder still as the queen brushed at her dress and took in the surrounding clearing. The paper king called back his sons and wrapped his protective arms around his wife as the angry whispers surged around them.

"Your father never had that much hair, and the youngest never grew that tall," the tutor breathed, reaching out to the king with the princes gathered on her palm, "but they captured your mother quite exactly."

The prince set the stag upon his shoulder where its antlers soon tangled in his hair, but at least he knew where it was. The royal couple stepped onto the old woman's hands, pulling their children close. The tutor lowered herself back down to better examined the family in the firelight, and the queen finally recognized her and stepped forward to show her the baby.

"Ah, not exactly at all," said the tutor, though she did so without disappointment. "Whoever drew your mother was very kind when they did, and they left out the limp when she walked." She looked down at the babe and smiled. "Hello, Your Highnesses. It has been quite some time."

But the prince no longer paid any attention, and he heard nothing of his mother's reply. Instead, he listened to years of sleepless nights while the queen paced the castle hallways. He knew the sound as well as anything, and he still awoke sweating in the night hearing it. It was regular and smooth like the tick of a clock echoing in the castle halls. There was no room for doubt in the prince's mind. The queen did not limp.

Pieces clicked together, one into the next. The queen not remembering the secret ways that wormed through the castle walls. The change of staff while the queen mourned her husband in a tower. Her own children barely recognizing her when she finally emerged. Each boy taking a trip, never to return—except the youngest who couldn't remember his mother's face at all.

And at the start, the voyage on which his father died with only one survivor returning.

The prince's mouth hung open as he looked around the clearing at the battered remnants of his kingdom. They watched the royal family as it stood on the old tutor's hands, unaware that something fundamental had changed, oblivious to the seismic shift they had witnessed. The prince's heart fluttered in his chest, and he sat heavily back on the hard forest floor.

"The queen is not my mother," the prince said, at first more to himself than to the others, "and so she's not the queen at all."

"What was that?" the tutor asked, looking away from her friend and the babe in her arms.

"The queen is an imposter and has been for years," the prince said, more firmly, looking up at everyone who towered above him. The only place he refused to look was the old tutor because standing in her hands was the small figure of his mother—a woman he couldn't remember knowing. "My parents died together, lost at sea one terrible night." The fury of it made him shake, and he felt like running all the way to the castle and beating against the gates until they fell.

"Nonsense," the older man said, "do you have any proof?"

But the prince shook his head. He had nothing.

He looked at the tutor whose eyes flared wide in the firelight and at the drawing of his mother, standing still and looking so hollow she might blow away. Whoever had replaced the queen had fooled the kingdom by removing anyone who might see through her. Now she sat upon the throne with her heightened walls and an immense army around her—and the prince's befuddled stepfather who'd funded it all sitting by her side.

"Then there is nothing to be done,' the older man continued. "She has beaten us, and we don't have the forces to retake the castle."

The prince looked around at the defeated faces in the flickering light and untangled the stag from his hair. It sat in his palm, panting and slowly wagging its tail.

"Maybe we do," the prince murmured, and then he smiled. He wasn't certain anyone would follow his commands, and so he made none. Instead, he met their eyes with his, looking from each to the next, and the prince made a request. "I need to ask you to do something for me."

And they did.

Gathering

ith that, a message travelled out across the kingdom from one hidden camp to the next, and then it spilled over the borders into neighbouring lands where the prince's subjects had fled from the iron fist of the queen. When news arrived, people searched houses and barns, towers and tombs, and called to their countrymen to step out of hiding. It was the most baffling call to action, a request to hearts instead of minds because it asked people to believe in something ludicrous.

People still came, and when they did, they brought books. Soon the camp spilled out of the forest, and the stacks of books created a semblance of streets and alleys.

With each new book, the prince coaxed the woodcuts and drawings awake with the magic book that rang in his head like a bell until the fields rustled with woodcuts flittering around the hundreds of men and women willing to raise up arms in one last fight for the kingdom. New people stumbled in each day with doubt in their hearts, but when they saw the force assembling before them, they skipped like children and embraced strangers like old friends.

When at last it came time to march, the air was full of dragons and insects, sea monsters, and paper birds, while the field was thick with tiny people and all manner of beasts as far as the eye could see. With them walked families and the old and the young carrying swords, pitchforks, and branches. At their centre walked the prince with his swirling book surrounded by a hundred stags serving his personal guard, including one that chased after laces and tripped on uneven legs. Before them, the queen's scouts and search parties fled. Those who reached her camps were laughed off as idiots and fools until the paper army crashed down upon them with a force of citizens at their backs.

But the journey was long, and the magic grew thin. Sometimes a creature crashed from the sky, or a beast seized on the road. Now when the prince looked at the book in his hands, it didn't always ring in his head like a bell. As the army moved forward, the prince lost count of the crumpled pages lost in the mud, stories that might never be heard again. Each time the prince had to wonder if it was one of his—a character he'd grown up with that would never return to the castle library to pass a rainy afternoon sat by the window.

On the third night, the prince called a meeting, and he gathered around him the wisest there were, pulled from the humans, the authors and the drawn.

The spirit of an author complained loudly, saying he couldn't rewrite without paper and ink. He was a wispy gentleman in a thick robe who held a book on candlewicking to his chest. Without supplies, there was no way to repair his book, he complained, but another author waved him away like smoke from a candle and the prince caught his book as it fell.

"I have only heard stories of magic books," said an elderly man who sat down where the author had been, "though none that behaved quite like this."

A paper-craft figure patted that man's knee, "They're difficult to make, and this one has done quite a lot. The risk now is pulling it too thin."

Next, the prince turned to the tutor who looked at the book with some thought. "I spent many long years in the castle library, and I have never seen this book," she said. Many of the royal books and the drawings within followed the tutor like old friends. "In fact, the only magic book I have ever seen was the one that belonged to the queen."

At this, the night grew quiet, and everyone leaned closer to the fire.

"I remember her book," the prince said. "It was about lineage and laws. It never interested me enough to learn more, but it was never out of the imposter's sight." He looked back to his own book which swirled silently on his lap.

The tutor nodded. "The true queen called it the Book of the Crown, but I never saw inside it. She kept it in the library with all the others, but said it was far too dry a read."

"But how was it magic?" the prince asked.

"It knows things," the tutor said with a shrug, "but what it knows I just couldn't say. I have spent my life in libraries from one coast on to the next. Never have I seen one with magic, yet apparently your library had two."

A paper-craft king stepped forward. and whoever had drawn him had included the book in question which he held up for all to see. "I wish I could tell you what was inside it," he said, sadly, "but it was with me throughout my rule, and that was centuries ago."

"Two magic books!" said another, though she had nothing else to add.

"Let's rest your book," the tutor said to the prince. "Call back your woodcuts and drawings. When we need them most, you can release them again, but until then let's let the magic sleep." There was a chorus of agreement, and so as the prince walked back to his tent in the darkness, he listened to the rustling army climbing back between its covers.

The next morning, the prince had to gape at how small their force had become. Where yesterday they had stretched from the forest to the lake, now they were eight hundred at best, each weighed down by as many books as they could carry.

"It will be all right," his father said from the prince's top pocket, but the prince paid him no mind. Whoever had written his father and drawn his face had seen the man as an optimist. Almost nothing got him down, even when it should. The prince wished he'd been written the same way, but, instead, the smile on his face was only skin deep as he greeted his people and rolled up his tent. The remnants of the kingdom's citizens went forth carrying books in carts and sacks, held in their arms and strapped to their sides. They were thin and sickly and the going was slow, but they were still buoyed by fresh hope after so many years of none.

The prince, on the other hand, worried. What if he called forth his paper army and the books didn't respond? What if they faced the queen's army alone? They would be slaughtered inside of an hour down to every last woman and man, leaving nothing but bloody books on the field.

Around him, people tried not to leave any paper behind, even books of math or childhood stories. Some staggered under the weight they bore, but no one wanted to reach the castle with one less page than necessary. They had a magic prince on their side, and that was a sign. They saw his intensity as he stared at his book, exchanged glances and continued preparing for the march. No one had met a magical prince before, so they didn't know what to expect. They gave him his peace.

The prince had no such spring for his confidence. His countrymen thought of magic against steel, tearing down the walls of the castle. But the prince thought of the queen's endless letters, torn open with the knife for the butter. In his pocket was the lifeless woodcut of a stag he'd accidentally crushed in his hands as a child. Paper could only do so much against swords. So far they'd had surprise on their side, but the ragtag army moved slowly and that advantage was fading.

He stared at the swirling cover as he strapped it to the roll of his tent. The book again rang in his head, but his doubts distracted him so that he barely saw what was before him and almost missed the change.

For a moment it had seemed like a cloud rolled across the cover and away. The prince saw the word "king" in the swirling ink and perhaps the word "prince," but then the cover settled back into chaos. His eyes stung and the bell in his head rose into a fury. The prince swayed, catching himself on the bundle of tent, and still trying to force the letters back into focus. The headache returned, and the word tipped precariously, but still, the prince did not look away.

Finally, he opened the magic book which now glowed with its pale, pink light. "I know you're in there," he whispered to the unreadable pages within.

After he'd met the first author, he'd tried this a hundred times more. It worked with some books, and the authors met him in the silvery guise of a spirit, critiquing his treatment of the works they'd composed. In others, the authors scurried away, deeper into their margins for privacy. In one case, the same author wrote several books, and his doubles surrounded the prince, each at a different stage in his career. They argued for a week until the prince sent them back into their bindings, though they still gossiped about each other whenever they were released.

But there had never been as much of a whisper from the author of the slim magic book, no matter how many times the prince asked.

"Please," he said, "I just want to know who you are."

The pages flickered as if a wind blew across them, and the ink churned.

It was getting late and people were restless to move, hoping to reach the castle with their magical army. Someone called the prince's name, and at the edges, the march had begun.

"Please," the prince repeated to the book, "the kingdom lives or dies today, and our chances are slim. I have been a child for too long and now find they need me to be a prince and not the drawing of one on a library rug with a paper sword in my hand."

His head felt like it would split apart, and he was ready to turn away. He couldn't let the book overpower him and leave him senseless for days. His people needed him, and if they waited much longer, the queen's forces would come.

"If I'm going to die today," the prince pleaded as he prepared to slam the book shut, "I want to know your story."

With that, the prince disappeared and the magic book dropped onto the rolled-up tent.

The Old King

The prince found himself standing on the castle's grand staircase, looking down at the main hall. The front doors stood open, letting in a warm summer breeze. Servants scurried past on the upper landing, carrying a basket of laundry between them, and they laughed in a way that the prince had only seen happen in books. Different paintings filled the walls, and where his father's had been, there was a portrait of a king and a queen together, both looking terribly smug.

Then there was a girl on the stairs, running down towards him. Her pink dress tangled her legs. She tripped beside him, and the prince caught her and swept her back to her feet. She was as light as sunshine as he set her down, and her smile was radiant. The prince smiled in return, and as she dashed away with a skip-jump stride, he chased along.

They wove through the grand hall and out past the throne room, down the wide hall of the western wing. At times he lost sight of her, but he followed her laughter up the servants' stairs. Before him, the library doors stood open, and the girl stopped in the doorway and then slipped inside and away.

The prince stopped to catch his breath, looking for the girl in the room he knew so well which was different in a thousand tiny ways, but she was gone.

Now it was night. A small fire burned in the fireplace, and the old lanterns hanging from the ends of the shelves were lit. Some books had changed, and one of the carpets. The painting above the mantle was an unfamiliar spray of flowers trailing along a stream that seemed to flow when the prince wasn't quite looking. He knew many of the books quite well, but somehow they seemed younger. Their spines weren't as worn, and the leather shone in the lamplight. Several windows opened to a cool evening breeze thick with the verdant scent of a garden.

"I think you've been looking for me," said a voice thick with age and light with illness, and when the prince turned, a king sat in the prince's favourite chair by the fire. The old man had the look of someone suddenly thin, an empty coat of a man, and his crown was ludicrously large on his head. He smiled and took it off, setting it down on the arm of the chair before flattening his wisps of hair and settling back into the cushions.

"It fit well when I was a stronger man," the king said, gesturing just so as he did. For a moment the prince pictured a crown like antlers branching up and away as he imagined this king in his prime.

"Who was that girl?" the prince asked. He stepped into the room, feeling the softness of the rug underfoot. He worried about his filthy feet, but when he looked down, they were clean.

"My daughter," the king murmured, and his wrinkled old face rolled up in a smile that told the prince all he needed to know. This man was like parents he'd met in the books, his own paper parents sleeping in his top pocket, and some of those who marched in the prince's army—they loved their children and that was all you needed to know. Suddenly the prince missed his stepfather dearly.

"Are you my grandfather?" the prince asked, settling onto a footstool before the king.

"I don't rightly know," the king replied, peering down his nose, "but the book answers to you, so it might be so."

"What's the book for?" the prince breathed as he'd asked himself countless times before. It was a tool that could build houses and tunnel through castle walls. It gave reality to creatures of myth and brought history to life. It could create armies that left generals shaking in fear and might even alter the course of a nation.

"Can't you yet tell?" The king laughed at his cleverness, and the prince realized he wasn't half as old as he seemed. He was ill—wasted, not wizened—but his eyes remained the vibrant blue of the young. The man's laughter descended into a wet cough, which wracked the king for quite some time, and when next he spoke, some of the man's spirit had faded. This author was dying, forever fading away within the book.

The king wiped at his mouth with a handkerchief before giving the prince an apologetic glance. "I wanted to tell stories to my daughter," the king murmured at last, and he wistfully looked out the window to the garden beyond.

"I spent my youth building a kingdom out of the ashes of the last, lost in quests and governance and finance, and then came a little girl who changed everything." He sighed before turning back to the prince. "Do you know I read to her on the night she was born and again every night that then followed? She couldn't sleep without a story in her ear, and to tell the truth, neither could I. A most unkingly thing indeed," the king said with a smirk before coughing again into the handkerchief. "The nursemaids thought I was mad."

The young man stood and poured the king a drink from the flagon by the fire, which the old man accepted gratefully. Spices swirled in the dark wine.

"They'll tell you the nursemaids know best," the king said raising his glass, but his voice darkened. "They'll also tell you a king's place is his throne. My own father died a stranger, having lived his life out in the world fighting battles. I kissed his ring at state dinners and wore black for months while pretending to mourn."

The prince nodded, but he felt awkward now that he saw the king's eyes were wet.

"But you cannot command sickness away, and even kings must end," the monarch continued. "I'd waited too long for children. She was so young, and I knew she would someday forget me."

The prince knew that feeling very well as he had no memory of his own father or brothers or even the queen before

84

the imposter. The king laughed again, wiping his eyes with the back of his hand.

"Does it seem so ludicrous? Is it so selfish? Of all the things magic can do, all the great wonders it can weave, a king wrote himself into a book so he might talk to his daughter in whatever small way he still could."

Once more, the king's eye wandered to the window and the garden beyond, and the prince sensed part of the monarch was out there with a small girl in pink. He listened to the tick of the mantle clock and the snap of the wood in the fire until the king's thoughts found their way back to the library.

The prince leaned forward and patted the king on the knee. "Well, I've liked every story you've told me, except perhaps the ones about math," the prince said. "You've kept me safe when by all rights I should not be, and you've given hope to an entire kingdom."

"Have I?" the king asked, quite surprised. He looked the prince up and down, from his bare feet to his threadbare tunic. "A slim hope if appearances are true."

The prince nodded and sagged. He'd come looking for a weapon, a magic big enough to change nations, and he'd ended up with stories instead. "A stranger has stolen the kingdom, and she cloaks herself as my mother the queen."

The king held the handkerchief to his mouth. "That won't do at all," he said with deepening concern.

"No," the prince agreed, shaking his head, "but I have no proof, and the magic of your book seems to fail. Even if I take back the throne, who will believe that my cause is just? What will prevent neighbouring countries from taking the throne? I had hoped you might help."

The king shook his head and sighed a rattling sigh. "All I can do is tell stories, My Prince. Bedtime stories for girls and kings who can't sleep." He looked thoughtful for a moment and then eased himself from his chair by the fire to stand on unsteady feet. The king rubbed his side as he scanned the shelf and selected a book that the prince knew well. It was the queen's book, the only book he left behind when he escaped the castle. It was a big, heavy tome edged in gold and engraved with a massive old oak.

"What you need," the king said, "is a family tree." He opened the cover and revealed a tree had been etched on the lining with branches that grew wide and long. There at the bottom of the lowest branch was the king's name and beneath it just one other—a name that caused the prince to smile.

"My mother," he said, rising and running a finger along it.

"Then I suppose I am your grandfather," the king said, beaming down at the prince, but then the smile faltered as the king realized what this news meant. For a moment, a question formed on his lips. He decided not to ask it, but his face grew pale. "But this isn't actually the book, and I'm not actually your grandfather. If it was, your name would be there, which might just be the proof that you need."

The prince nodded and reached out a hand to touch the old man's arm, which was more bone than anything else. "Then I know what I need to do," the prince said.

He bowed to the king and ran from the room, out into the hall and beyond, and a moment later he found himself again on the field where his people were beginning their march. On his lap was the swirling book, but the cover was no longer hard to read. "A King's Book for His Princess, the Most Beautiful Girl in the World." The book thrummed as the old king readied for the battle ahead, a battle for a kingdom and for family, and it rang in the prince's head like an army.

Siege

As the citizens marched, the leaders of the ragtag force met with the prince, and the adults tried to tell him what to do. The prince just shook his head. "I have my own plans," he stated, and he unstrapped the tent from his back and discarded it. Tonight he would sleep in his old castle bed or else he would never sleep again. On the horizon, he already saw the tallest tower and when the wind shifted, it carried distant castle drums.

There was a grumble as many had lost any patience they had left for royalty, but the prince carried a magic book that was the only way to carry the day, so they listened to the young man's instructions about the castle's weaknesses and the advantages of the surrounding ruins. He pointed out places where the outer wall was weak and locations of various tunnels that might still be intact. He described the effects of the sun and where it might blind the castle's defenders, as well as how to run when archers searched for targets. The prince contained the knowledge of a thousand books, and the people listened with growing respect.

When the castle appeared on the horizon, the prince handed several empty covers to the tutor. "You don't have to go alone," she said, reaching out to embrace him as she likely had with his brothers. The prince shook his head and stepped away. His brothers were dead, and the only person he wanted to embrace was his stepfather, who was hopefully alive and well inside the castle.

One by one, he took his family from his top pocket and set them atop of the tutor's stack. The figure of his mother was the last to let go of his hand, and the prince wished he had known her in life. Whoever had drawn her designed a queen the prince would have loved, and he lingered with the warmth of her hands on his finger. When he turned away, she called out, but the prince did not look back.

He took with him the travelogue and his grandfather's magic book, and he stuffed his pockets with as many stags as he could carry before setting off into the forest. The ragtag army marched forward along the road looking small and forlorn, but the books they carried were already waking, unfolding creatures of nightmares and small paper soldiers, mythical beasts and villagers. Before the castle disappeared entirely behind the trees, the prince counted the cannons being rolled into place atop the distant walls. Cannons terrified soldiers and knocked siege engines aside in a flash, but they meant little to paper. The real danger would come later.

The workers had left many hours before, and the prince followed the path they'd marked on the trees. He met up with some of the contingent, one of whom turned to him to report. "As expected, the queen resealed the tunnels, but we have opened a path, Your Highness." She looked at the prince appraisingly and rested her shovel against her hip. "You're much taller than you used to be but should fit if you don't breathe too deep." She bowed, and the prince followed her down into a hole in the forest floor.

And just like that, the prince was back inside the walls of the castle, being waved at by supportive woodcuts who made way as he passed. The walls shook as the cannon fire began, and the sound was even worse than the prince remembered from his childhood. This time he knew who was being fired upon, both the living and the enchanted, and it caused the prince to crawl even faster than before.

The path emerged in the kitchens, and servants stumbled back as the prince unfolded himself from the loose panel in the wall. He unstrapped the books from his back and emptied his pockets of stags, scattering them across the broad kitchen table. The stags climbed to their hooves, and servants ran screaming as the travelogue unravelled the history of the kingdom across the floury tabletop.

"Find the book," the prince whispered, and with an explosion of wings and claws, hooves and fins, the pages spread out to search the castle. The prince plucked up the dog-like stag as it tried to keep up with its brothers and tucked it into his pocket before he too padded off on his way. In each room, he tested his passageways until he found one that opened before him, and like that he was again in the walls.

Woodcuts

It was a far tighter fit than he'd remembered, and where he'd once run like a thief in the night, now he shuffled carefully along, catching on sharp twisted nails and ragged bits of brick. Outside the battle had started, and cannon fire shook the world. There was a crash as a castle wall caved in, and the prince smiled at the work of his tunnellers. The pink light of his grandfather's book was all the prince had as he listened for a sound of the queen, but the glow had already grown dimmer.

All at once there was a cacophony from the eastern wing. The prince scurried towards the clash of metal against stone and the screaming, but when he arrived in the second parlour, he found the queen's guards on the rug. His pages had been there already.

Half of a dragon lay still on a sofa. The prince bent to pick it up, but as he did, his eye fell upon the window.

Word of the books must have gotten back to the castle. The soldiers on what remained of the wall fired arrows tipped in fire, and the prince saw nothing but a wall of flame and smoke from beyond.

These rooms were much smaller than the prince remembered, but all at once he felt like a boy as he swallowed back a catch in his throat. All he could do was watch the smoke rise and pool against the dome of the sky, carrying the ash of his friends away.

There were screams as well, and the horrified prince remembered that the books weren't fighting alone.

And then he heard the beastly calls echoing through the halls. First, the roar of a dragon and then the squawking of birds. The prince raced towards the throne room, past broken guards and the weeping angles of the butler who huddled beneath a table. When he burst through the grand throne room doors, the frenzy staggered the prince to a stop.

A thousand paper figures advanced on the queen. She backed towards the throne with her book in her hands, not quite so tall as the prince remembered. Her crown lay battered and bent on the floor, and her bell-shaped dress was torn in a dozen place. Nearby, the prince's stepfather grinned in wonder as all manner of beasts flitted around him and laughed as an eagle landed upon his nose.

The paper was so thick that the queen appeared in glimpses. Older than he remembered, more crooked and bent. It took several moments for the prince to see her, the ageing queen with the cruel eyes and the beautiful witch crackling magic, and both were true together. Finally, the prince stepped forward and caught her eye, and both of her faces smiled as one.

She focussed again, settling back into the guise of the queen.

"Do you know what paper does really quite well?" she called to him above the rustling before raising a hand to her heart. Suddenly fire burst forth, catching the paper-craft figures so that they trailed through the air like comets, and the prince stumbled forward to catch them but only grabbed ash from the air. The prince's stepfather yelled in fright and tumbled to the ground, beating at the flames showering down upon him.

"No," the prince yelled, leaping toward the old man, but with another flip of the queen's hand, the prince fell and slid back across the floor. He hit the wall and lost the air from his lungs, but he held tight to his grandfather's book.

Suddenly everything grew quiet, save for the muffled fighting outside. The prince raised up his head, and the room swam around him. He gulped at the air in big, ragged gasps.

The queen laughed a doubled laugh, both queen and witch, and she set down her book on the throne. Then there was the smooth even stride he knew so well from years of hearing her pace in the night.

"Another magic book," she said sweetly as she walked towards him, "and you thought you could defeat me with drawings." She tsked and glanced over at his stepfather, who lay on the ground still patting frantically at his smoking tunic. "Husband, our beloved son has finally come home."

The prince raised himself up on his elbows, trying to shuffle back with nowhere to go.

The old man's brows knitted together as he sat up. Even when the old man's faculties failed him, he'd always recognized the prince. This time the young man saw nothing—just the confused look of a lost man in a senseless world as ash rained down around him.

"I know who you are," the prince said, looking back to the imposter and easing himself to his feet. "Or rather, I know who you aren't," he said with more certainty.

The queen laughed again. "Oh, please say." She motioned over her shoulder to her husband, "He won't remember anything either way. You see, my spells are far better than yours." At that, she blew at a mote of ash, and it floated towards the prince, dancing weightlessly in the air.

The queen then reached out, and despite all the prince's strength, his magic book flew to her hand where its pink light flickered and died. She raised an eyebrow and smirked. "The most beautiful girl in the world," she read, but the book didn't respond. It didn't swirl, and the prince heard no ringing in his head. The queen opened the cover and flipped through the blank pages.

There was a rustling in the prince's top pocket, and he glanced down at the dog-like stag as it struggled to get free. An antler was broken, but it seemed otherwise fine. The prince clamped a hand over it, careful not to crush it further.

"I guess this story's over," said the queen, dropping the empty book to her side. "How did you like the ending?" She smirked once again, and the prince saw the witch peer out through the queen's eyes. He could see a slim resemblance to the drawing he knew as his mother, but it was stretched by the witch within until it was almost impossible to recognize. The prince understood why she'd had to send so many people away all those years ago.

"I wondered why you'd taken the library," she said, turning away and walking towards the throne. The bell of her dress swung through the ash, leaving a snake's path behind her.

The prince plucked the dog-stag from his top pocket and whispered to it quickly before dropping it to his side. He ran to his stepfather and wiped ash from his face, but still, there was no recognition. The old man's eyes were cloudy, and he seemed like nothing but bones in the prince's arms.

"What have you done to him?" the prince demanded, holding his stepfather tightly.

The queen stopped and turned, just steps from her throne. "Oh, not everyone can take a trip," she replied, "not when there's an army to fund."

At the edge of the room, the prince saw a white flash of movement but he did not turn to watch it. The stag stumbled on uneven legs, and its broken antler caught in the curtains. It tumbled to the ground like a whisper, and the boy was certain the queen would notice, but she gave no sign that she did. There was a scream from the castle grounds, and the queen drank it in like sweet wine.

"I'm told it's the last of the resistance," she said a moment later. "And just about time. A war is awfully expensive, my son, but I knew you would bring it to an end as princes are wont to do." She looked the prince over and seemed unimpressed by what she saw. "You simply can't help it—the story writes itself."

Finally, the queen sat upon the throne, pressing her book between her bell-shaped dress and the arm of the chair.

"They told me you'd died," she continued. "Many thought you kidnapped for a ransom, but the royal book knew you were all right. It counts princelings the way it does gold and knights and wheels of cheese in the larder."

The prince rose and stepped away from his stepfather, knowing whatever happened, he didn't want the old man caught in the middle. He glanced at his grandfather's book and then back at the queen, not knowing which way to run.

But by looking at them, he wasn't looking at the terrier-like stag as it made its way to the corner and then slowly lowered to its belly and crept towards the throne. For once the prince was happy with his childish drawing because the stag walked on the soft, silent pads of a dog's paws rather than the sharp, clattering hooves of a stag.

"Do I even need to ask you why?" the prince asked, biding his time. "Why my mother and why my family?"

"Do you?" the queen replied. "Isn't a throne enough?"

"I wouldn't know," said the prince. "I've never wanted one."

The stag reached the foot of the throne, and it began to climb the queen's dress, light as a petal and so small it had no trouble digging its paws into the lace.

Woodcuts

Despite the clumsiness of its design, the stag was still a reflection of its source—the wise old stag from the travelogue who had first guided the prince through the history of the world. That itself was the reflection of something else— something bigger and important enough that the prince had met it so many times as it climbed out of hundreds of books.

"What good is a ruined kingdom?" the prince asked, pacing off to the left so the queen would look away from the drawing climbing up her dress. It had tangled its remaining antler and was trying to pull itself free.

The witch queen snorted, brushing ash away from her cleavage. "A thousand times as much as no kingdom at all," she concluded. "Now, would you like to drown or to burn? To fall or to sicken?" She stood up again, and for a moment the prince saw her sickening smile spread down to her second face. He did not look away for fear he might look at the stag, which had just leapt onto the cushion of the throne. "Perhaps something new, like an arrow that gets traced back to some farmer's bow?" She cackled at this, and the prince's stomach soured to see the queen so victorious.

"I choose old age," the prince replied, stepping tentatively to his left. As he got too close to his grandfather's book, the queen's hand flipped up, and he found he could no longer move. Even breathing took every bit of strength the prince still had remaining.

"My apologies," the queen said, "I won't offer you that."

And as the queen took another step from the throne, the dog-stag slipped into the royal book and unfolded, releasing a puff of the king's pink magic. The queen spun around as the book creaked awake, sending out branches and roots that wrapped around the golden throne. Small plaques with royal names hung from each limb. It didn't grow tall and it didn't grow deep before the dog-stag's magic exhausted itself and the tree's growth shuddered to a stop.

The queen stared for a moment and then turned back to the prince, still frozen in her magic spell. "What was that supposed to do?" she cackled, and the prince swallowed hard, trying not to let his disappointment show upon his face.

"Give it a moment," the prince said through clenched teeth, fighting her spell enough to show a smirk of his own. The queen squinted, before slowly turning back to the tree on the throne, which did absolutely nothing at all.

With her attention diverted, the prince felt a slight crack in the spell that held him. He felt like his skin was tearing and his legs burned as he summoned all of his will to move—and he did, just a bit. He didn't manage a step or a leap to the side, but what he did was to inch a foot forward, leaving his weight to do the rest. Still frozen, the prince tipped backwards, smashing his head against the stone.

The queen turned at the sound, and as she did the tree upon the throne exploded outward until it scraped the high ceiling above and its roots cracked their way between the great stones of the floor. Branches exploded outward, thrashing at the queen, and she tumbled towards the prince who still lay on his back. His head rang from the fall, but even that was overpowered by the last of the magic in his grandfather's book. It lay pressed beneath the prince's shoulder spilling out pink light that swirled around the family tree that writhed around the room.

The prince rolled to his side, suddenly free. He dodged a plaque of his own name with the title of king and clutched at his head. Then he grabbed his grandfather's book just as a giant root slammed down, cracking the thick stone tiles. Somewhere in the deafening tumult, the prince heard his stepfather cry out, and the boy yelled for the tree to protect him.

The branches of his ancestors split before him, and the prince dodged his way to his stepfather's side. Somewhere fire flashed, but the tree was growing faster than the queen burned it away. The royal book had recorded countless generations, and for every limb that burned, three more arose, battering at the witch and bursting out windows, knocking knights and cannons from the castle walls and growing towards the dome of the sky.

The prince watched as the pink light in his hands flickered out once more. Abruptly the tree contracted, folding in on itself as the castle's roof collapsed and many walls tumbled down until it was just a book on the cushion of a broken throne. There was no sign of the imposter queen at all.

"Oh my," said the old man, whose eyes were now clear and creased at the edges with a familial pride. The prince pressed his forehead against his stepfather's shoulder. "How tall you've gotten," the old man murmured, and he wrapped his arms around the young prince.

Endings

When the tutor found them, the king sat in the kitchen eating day-old bread with his stepfather while he told the old man stories. A childish drawing of a stag was unfolded between them. She immediately bowed before the king motioned for her to rise, and then they offered her a crust to eat.

Soon they followed her to the castle wall where wounded needed care and dead needed burial. Burnt and tattered pages were matted in the mud and danced in the wind. Mostly, he spoke to surgeons and generals, blacksmiths and diplomats, and together they began to piece the kingdom back together.

A third of the citizens who'd marched that day had died, and barely half the pages crawled back to their books. The authors did what they could to rewrite the missing pages, but three days later when the last of the magic faded, many chapters remained missing. On that final night, the king didn't sleep. Instead, he sat with his brothers at the top of the highest tower, staring up at the stars until the princes quietly unfolded beside him.

For many weeks, the king couldn't think of books, not even the royal book. When there came a time he needed to consult the laws, he found the family tree had changed. It now featured the drawing of a witch tangled within its roots.

Years later, when the king had children of his own, he read to them, filling in the missing pages with words of his own. When his daughters grew old enough, they were often found in the library, without either of their fathers coaxing them or their step-grandfather by their side.

The king's eldest liked stories of swordplay or the newer books about a witch queen and a stag. The middle like poems that rhymed, and she memorized them all by heart and held recitations that lasted well past her bedtime.

The youngest was drawn to anything with pictures and couldn't be bothered with text at all.

One day the king found her reading a slim book, a book about the most beautiful girl in the world. He knelt down to join her only to find she wasn't reading the book at all. She was watching the pages as they so slowly swirled and listened as it rang in her head like a bell.

About the Author

Scott is a graduate of York University's Creative Writing program and works in the field of broadcast traffic, which has nothing to do with road congestion. He writes, performs and edits the Fairy Tales for Unwanted Children podcast from the hallway between his bathroom and kitchen. This helps reduce some of the noise of downtown Toronto, which has everything to do with road congestion. He has a cat.

To hear the podcast for free, please visit www.unwantedchildren.ca or search for the show on any podcasting app.

To link directly to the Woodcuts recordings, visit www.periodically.ca/woodcuts.